GILL JEPSON

OUT OF
TIME

The S_____ of the ____ Swan

GILL JEPSON

OUT OF TIME

The Secret of the Swan

Matador
5 Weir Road
Kibworth Beauchamp
Leicester LE8 0LQ, UK
Tel: (+44) 116 279 2299
Fax: (+44) 116 279 2277
Email: books@troubador.co.uk
Web: www.troubador.co.uk/matador

ISBN 978 1848766 129

British Library Cataloguing in Publication Data.
A catalogue record for this book is available from the British Library.

Typeset in 11pt Palatino by Troubador Publishing Ltd, Leicester, UK
Printed and bound in Great Britain by TJI Digital, Padstow, Cornwall

For the real George
1923-2004

CHAPTER 1

CHANGES

Rebecca hugged her knees, squeezing herself as small as she could, trying to disappear completely. She sighed heavily and shook her head, trying to clear her mind, hoping to shake out all the worries wriggling in her brain like little worms. It was no good. The thoughts wouldn't disappear. She uncurled and sprang like a cat onto the grass. She stood and stretched, angry feelings fizzing and crackling like a firework inside her tummy. She scowled as she spotted the groundsman waving at her from the other side of the cloister. Why did *he* look so happy?

She strode off down the bank towards the abbey church, kicking tufts of grass as she went. This was *her* special place; they used to come here all the time. It was a wonderfully magical place, but that had soon changed.

She spun around quickly when she heard the shrill call of her best friend Megan. Rebecca sighed impatiently. Could she have no peace at all? Under normal circumstances she would have been thrilled to see her friend, but these weren't normal circumstances. She groaned inwardly when she saw that Megan was not alone. She had that new boy in tow again. Well, she didn't *have* to make friends if she didn't feel like it. Who did he think he was anyway, coming to *her* abbey?

The two children raced across the grass unaware of Rebecca's hostility.

"Hi!" breezed Megan.

Something like a low growl escaped from Rebecca's lips.

Danny, oblivious to the unfriendly welcome, grinned amiably at her.

She gritted her teeth and did not return the smile.

"Phaw! Who's rattled your cage?"

This irritated Rebecca even more. She turned her back on him sulkily.

"What's up, Becca?" asked Megan, placing a kindly hand onto her shoulder.

The gesture confused Rebecca. She didn't want anyone to be kind and she didn't want to have to be kind back. Her eyes prickled with hot, stinging tears. Trying to blink them back, she rubbed her eyes roughly.

"Are you crying?" asked Megan.

"NO!" snapped Rebecca.

"You are!" insisted Danny.

The tears came spilling down her hot, red cheeks and the anguish escaped in a terrible howl of unhappiness.

Danny put his arm round her and Megan pulled her down onto the grass to sit with them. They sat together in silence for some time until Rebecca had cried her last tear.

Gradually, over the following weeks Danny, Megan and Rebecca became inseparable. Soon it was hard to tell that Danny was a newcomer. In fact it had been strangely helpful that he *was* new and he hadn't known how things were before it had all gone wrong. Their favourite haunt was Bow Bridge and the Vale of the Deadly Nightshade. At first Rebecca wanted to keep it all for herself. It was hard to let other people into her private world; after all she hardly knew Danny.

The abbey was incredible. Once inside they played hide and seek, climbed and explored the ruins, made up games of knights, castles and dragons. They knew that you shouldn't climb on ancient monuments, but somehow that made it even more fun. It wasn't as if they could damage the ruins – after all they had been there since 1123, which seemed a very long time to them!

Rebecca was glad she had decided to share her special place with Megan and Danny. It was never going to be the same as when she and her best and loveliest granddad used to walk amongst the ruins; but in a funny way, she had a warm, comfortable feeling when they were with her.

Every thing had changed so quickly that summer. Granddad had a stroke. He looked the same, but whatever the stroke thing had done it must have been big because he had to go to hospital in an ambulance. Rebecca had been scared to visit, in case he didn't get better. Confused thoughts and worries scurried round her mind like mice. It was like that game you played where you don't step on the cracks in a pavement in case it really did give you bad luck!

When she did visit, he waved at her from the chair next to his bed and smiled his lovely smile, the one that shone right up to his twinkly, blue eyes. The shock came when he spoke.

Granddad spoke backwards! All his words were jumbled up. He got cross with himself when he couldn't say what he wanted to, but laughed when her brothers teased him about it.

Rebecca couldn't believe it when the doctor said Granddad could go home. She had bubbles of excitement inside when they went to collect him from the hospital. The two of them smiled at each other on the way home. Soon things would be back to normal…she was sure!

The bowl shaped amphitheatre was strange. Rebecca's Granddad had told her that it was made when the monks were quarrying the sandstone for the abbey and they made a fish pond in the base for the brothers. It had an eerie, strange atmosphere even when you knew what it really was. As somewhere to play, it was anything you wanted it to be. In winter it became the Cresta Sledge Run, in summer, a football pitch or a climbing wall and it was also a great place to have a picnic.

The friends spent more and more time investigating the abbey grounds. The groundsman waved from different parts of the abbey and seemed to appear wherever they were. Rebecca and Megan knew him from school trips and knew he could tell stories about the abbey. On one particularly hot afternoon, they had gone behind the huge walls of the ruined church to get some shade. The tall ruins of the chancel and nave threw strong shadows across the grass. They lay on the springy grass, chatting and lazing through the long, hazy afternoon.

"It used to be a cemetery here, you know?" Rebecca commented. She felt a pang as she said it.

Megan sat up and shrugged her shoulders with a small shiver, "Ugh! You could've told us!"

"Well, you could've guessed, there are grave stones all over the place " said Danny.

They all looked around, to confirm what he had said.

"Oh yeah! I never noticed before, I thought they were just stones!"

They were not all immediately recognisable as gravestones. They were different sizes, shapes and styles. A couple of them had small body shaped indentations and one had a simple cross marked along its full length. The new discovery prompted them to start examining them in more detail. Danny tried out the body shapes by lying in them.

"This can't be right – a man wouldn't fit in here!" shouted Danny. "It only just fits me!"

"DUH! "exclaimed Rebecca," They were smaller in those days!"

Danny scrambled from his resting place, "Well, they must've been bloody midgets then!"

"Well, they were smaller than we are today," an unfamiliar voice broke in. They turned round quickly. It was the groundsman, recognisable by his white English Heritage helmet and green overalls. He had appeared silently, suddenly, out of thin air!

"They didn't have our rich diet, so they weren't as tall as we are". He talked to them as though he had known them personally, for years. Oddly enough, Megan and Danny began to feel as though they had known *him* for years, too. Rebecca remained aloof.

"Do you know a lot about history then?" asked Danny.

"Oh you know, you pick up odds and ends in this job," he replied.

"I bet you know lots about this place, don't you?" pressed Danny, "Gruesome murders, ghosts and hidden treasure an' all that. I bet there's tons of that stuff here!"

"Oh, I wouldn't go that far, but I do know things that aren't common knowledge," he said, with a half smile.

"Brill!" Danny was jumping up and down and punching the air with excitement, "Go on then! Tell us! What secrets? Go on!"

"Oh yes! Go on, tell us!" shouted Megan. The excitement was infectious.

Rebecca stood quietly by. She was reluctant to include yet *another* person in her special place. "I bet he doesn't know as much about the abbey as my Granddad anyway!" she thought. She watched him with detachment.

"Well, I've a tea break due," he said looking at his wrist watch," I suppose I can spare a few minutes. "

"Huh! We'll never get rid of him!" thought Rebecca.

The man stood feet apart, hand holding his chin, as though he was considering a weighty problem. Slowly, he began nodding his head.

"Well, I can tell you about the abbey treasure…or at least begin."

"I knew it!" yelled Danny jubilantly. "I knew there'd be treasure!"

"Hmmm! There's treasure…and *treasure!*" he said, mysteriously.

Megan and Danny waited for him to speak, hardly

daring to breathe. Rebecca pretended not to be interested. The groundsman was a picture of calmness and peace, almost as if time was standing still and his 15 minute tea break would be endless. He didn't move for what seemed an age. Then, he suddenly galvanised into action and marched off towards a small, sandstone grave marker, sunken into the soft grass and moss. Megan and Danny looked at each other and followed him, Rebecca reluctantly joined them.

"Few people know about this, so be careful who you tell. I found it, one morning, when I was trimming the grass...and this really *is* a treasure!"

He knelt down and the children dropped to their knees too. He lovingly brushed back the grass bordering the edge of the stone at its base.

"Here, take a look..." As he folded back the grass, the children peered closely at the stone. Rebecca forgot her bad mood and caught her breath in wonder as he revealed a beautiful, carefully carved image, standing proud on the flat edge of the stone. It was a detailed, delicate, perfectly fashioned swan.

She reached out to trace the detailed outline and could almost feel the feathers. Around its long neck, was a garland of small flowers, so accurate that she could count the petals. The image mesmerised her and she became lost in thought, marvelling at how anyone could carve such a realistic image from stone. Suddenly her train of thought was shattered.

"I didn't expect a *duck!*" said Danny, disappointed. "I mean it's good, but its not *treasure* not *really!*"

"Oh it's gorgeous, Danny!" exclaimed Rebecca,

"And it's not a duck – it's a swan! Trust a boy not to be impressed!"

"No!" he explained, "I *am* impressed, but it's just not what I expected, that's all."

"I *did* say," interrupted the groundsman, "There's treasure…and there's *treasure!*"

"It means some'ing, don't it?" Danny addressed the groundsman directly.

"Oh yes!" he agreed, "But it will only reveal itself to those who can see!"

He turned and looked at his watch.

"Well! Better get on…" He strolled towards his hut on the rise of the hill.

"Hey! You can't leave it like that! What does it mean?" shouted Danny.

He turned slowly and smiled, waving back at them.

"Oh don't go!" cried Rebecca, "You haven't told us anything yet. We don't even know what to call you." She regretted her churlish behaviour earlier.

He stopped. "You can call me Mason. That'll do. Everyone calls me that."

With that he disappeared into his hut, closing the door. They looked at each other, exasperated.

"Let's go and talk to him some more. Come on!" encouraged Danny.

As they ran to the hut, Rebecca said "I didn't know they still used this, Granddad said they took your money in there and there was an old stove to keep them warm."

"Well he won't need a stove today, it's boiling!" Danny commented.

"I bet they've given it to Mason to put his tools and hat in," Megan added.

"Yeah! 'Cos you pay your money in the museum now!" agreed Danny.

They reached the hut, the door was shut fast.

"God! He must be sweltered in there in this heat! It's only a little hut ain't it?"

He knocked on the door and waited. No answer. He knocked again, a little harder. Still, there was no reply. "Mason! Come on! We won't go till you tell us!" cried Danny.

Ten minutes elapsed and the door remained shut. Danny reached for the handle, "He's locked it!" he stated obviously.

"Yes, but look!" gasped Rebecca, pointing at the door.

A large padlock hung from the hasp, on the outside.

"But we saw him go in!" said Megan in a puzzled tone.

"He *did* go in!" added Danny.

There was no obvious sign of escape – and why would he want to escape anyway?

"It's weird! He went in. We could see him clearly all the way up the hill and there's nowhere else he could have gone."

If they were puzzled now, this was nothing to their astonishment the next time they saw him.

Chapter 2

Discoveries

Granddad settled back at home and things appeared to be back to normal. Rebecca called in every day to keep him company. He had become quiet and thoughtful; she thought this might be because his speech was still strange and muddled.

On Thursday it was very hot. Granddad had changed into his shorts and put on his sun hat. Rebecca joined him in the back garden and they sat quietly together on the bench. Rebecca basked in the sunshine and smiled to herself. "He's going to be alright, I know it."

She looked at him; he had nodded off, his chin resting on his chest. She watched his chest go up and down steadily and the rhythm of his breathing was comforting. Like a clock ticking…in …out…in…out…tick…tock…tick…tock.

She smiled smugly and hugged his arm. He stirred for a second, muttering under his breath. She couldn't tell what he was saying at first.

"Stone…the stone. Go gone Sid! Brother is he?"

She sat up and looked at him closely. He looked troubled. Suddenly, he waved his arms about as if he was swatting an invisible insect.

"Me head…creatures…Mam! MAM! Scratchin' murkies, hide…crawlers …sign at them looking!"

"Granddad!" cried Rebecca in alarm.

He woke abruptly and both of them jumped. He looked at her as if he had never seen her before, his eyes as round as two blue buttons. Gradually, the recognition returned to his eyes and he smiled. Rebecca smiled back, a little uncertainly.

The weather changed. Big black clouds rolled in off the Irish Sea and brought thunder and spectacular bolts of lightening with them. She felt afraid. Not just because of the thunderstorm. Something else was frightening, but she couldn't tell what...

The mystery of Mason's disappearance plagued them. Rebecca knew what they had seen, but could not explain his disappearance. There was something special about the groundsman. By three o'clock the next day, they could contain their curiosity no longer. They decided to return to the abbey and sped down the fields to Bow Bridge and across the path to the railway crossing. When they reached the abbey museum, they paused in the entrance, panting and gasping for breath in the heat.

They paid their money and bought an ice lolly to quench their thirst. The ticket lady smiled, "My word, you do like this abbey! What on earth are you hoping to find?" she continued. She stared and smiled very intensely. Rebecca felt a shiver ripple down her back.

"Er nothing really..."

The woman continued to beam, the smile stretching across her face almost unnaturally.

"I'm sure there's *something* you're looking for dear," she insisted.

Rebecca grinned nervously and shook her head.

"You can tell me, dear. This old abbey has many

hidden secrets… and you children wheedle your way into nooks and crannies… I know, I've watched you!"

Rebecca stared at her, motionless, unable to speak.

The smile vanished from the woman's face, her features freezing into a scowl like one of the abbey's gargoyles.

Abruptly she turned away.

"Well off you go! I can't spend all day talking to you!"

Danny shrugged and led the girls to the steps outside.

"Well *that* was weird," whispered Megan as they walked down the steps.

The view was panoramic. They could see the cemetery, where they had talked to Mason yesterday and in the distance, the old custodian's hut.

They retraced their steps and ran down the green slope. Megan found the stone first. She was bending over it. Danny and Rebecca peered at the stone.

"Well!" said Rebecca, "are we going to look then? Or do you think we imagined it all?"

Simultaneously, they knelt down and reverently folded back the grass around the edge of the stone. They all held their breath in suspense and gasped at the sight of the symbol, as they had yesterday.

"So, we didn't imagine it then!" Danny said, delightedly.

"What do we do next? Should we see if we can find Mason?"

The door of the custodian's hut was still locked. Danny rattled it, just to check.

"Well, what can we do now? We don't have any clues," interjected Danny. "How can you solve a puzzle without the clues?"

"Should we buy a guide book, it might help?" asked Rebecca. "I don't know how much money I've got with me." She pulled her purse out of her pocket and opened it, tipping it out. They counted out £1.92 in small change.

"I don't think that's enough. History books cost more than that!" said Rebecca.

Megan added another £1.50.

"Sorry, it's not much, but I bought a comic," she said apologetically.

"Still not enough!" said Rebecca. They looked pointedly at Danny, who had not yet offered his contribution. He sighed and emptied out his pockets. He pulled out a variety of objects, the usual junk; stickers, chewing gum, string, football cards and coins.

He managed to contribute £2.

"Well, that's £5.42 that should do it," Rebecca said.

They browsed in the museum shop. Eventually, Rebecca found an illustrated volume which held a lot of information. While the girls paid for the book, Danny looked at the museum exhibits, suddenly, he let out a cry.

"Look! Quick!" He beckoned them to join him. There was an image of an illuminated manuscript, much enlarged and pressed between sheets of Perspex. The primitive picture depicted a monk, sitting at a writing slope, pen in hand, looking straight at them. His figure was bounded by a huge illuminated letter, the gold casting an eerie light onto his face. At his feet was a carefully drawn swan.

"Oh my God!" exclaimed Rebecca "It's like the swan on the grave stone! What does it say about it?"

They turned to the black script which accompanied the manuscript. Rebecca read it out aloud.

"This illuminated manuscript is taken from the Furness Coucher Book, which is now in the British Museum, the Coucher Book recorded the daily business in the Cistercian Abbey of St Mary of Furness, saved by the Abbot at the Reformation and is a unique history of the abbey. The picture of the monk is extremely unusual, as the scribe did not as a matter of course depict himself.

His name is John Stell and he lived in the abbey during the 15th century, working in the Scriptorium. Nobody knows why he felt important enough to insert himself into such a significant work. Equally, there has been much scholarly controversy over the significance of the swan at the base of the letter."

The children were silent.

"This is our first clue. The beginning of our quest!" said Danny excitedly.

"Even if we don't know what the "quest" is! And each time we find something out, a new question pops up!" added Rebecca.

They began reading the screens and posters. The information was abundant. How much of it would be relevant was unsure.

"This is no good," said Megan, "We'll never remember all this!"

CHAPTER 3

A PROMISE 1415

John Stell had just woken, dawn was breaking and it was time to go to Prime, the first service of the day. Next would be the Chapter House, to hear a chapter read from the Rule of St Benedict. The abbey business would be discussed and he would be told his duties for the day.

Daily, Brother John worked as a scribe and each day he thanked God for giving him work that he truly loved. The abbot had instructed the monks to copy all the charters and abbey documents and John found it interesting work. He loved to create beautiful illuminated letters and each day when he put down his quill, he surveyed his work with a warm glow of pleasure. Almost instantly, guilty thoughts overcame him for being so proud of his work. He knew pride was a sin, but he couldn't help himself.

The abbot, William of Dalton, the prior and the subprior who directed work in the Scriptorium, were standing in front of John Stell. The other monks had departed as the abbot had requested. Brother John was nervous, he was trying to think of anything he may have done to deserve this level of attention from the senior monks in the abbey. He hoped they had not discovered that he had sneaked into the warming room yesterday; there were strict times when the monks were allowed to take advantage of the only heated room in the abbey. Surely, that would not warrant such a reaction, he knew of others that had done the same thing without trouble. His worried thoughts were interrupted by the calm and measured voice of the abbot.

"Brother John, you have worked in the Scriptorium for some years now. We have seen the careful way you have executed your work."

John cursed himself. He knew now, it must be his sin of pride, after all he had only yesterday congratulated himself on the work he had completed on the Coucher Book. Before he could speak and begin to ask for forgiveness, the abbot continued.

"You are a skilled scribe and your illuminated lettering is unsurpassed in this abbey. You are devoted in your worship and your studies and we know you care about the ancient books in the library," he paused, waiting for a response.

John Stell, puzzled, yet at the same time relieved, silently agreed with what the abbot had just said.

"We have a task for you of great importance. You are loyal and trusted, but to undertake this task you must promise to be loyal to the very end of your existence. It is a weight which will be hard to bear, as there are those who would try to prevent you from keeping your vow. You will have to protect a treasure against all manner of rogues and ensure its safety through many events. We have chosen you for your good heart and you in turn must entrust others with the burden of protecting the treasure. How say you?"

Brother John gaped at them, hardly knowing what to think. He was flattered by their trust in him, yet baffled at what treasure they would entrust to his care.

"I will do all I can to protect any abbey treasure, but I do not know of what you speak," he replied.

The men smiled and nodded to each other, pleased that their estimation of him had been true.

"The treasure is hidden within the abbey and will be revealed to you in time. It is not *abbey* treasure, it belongs to all and its importance is so great that many with evil intentions wish to steal it," remarked the prior.

"You will be shown how to protect it and you will know those who can be trusted. There will be times in the future when it will be difficult to protect and when its true value will be disregarded in favour of greed and avarice. You will be its custodian and there will be others to help, if you are you willing to take on this task, no matter how long it takes?" added the abbot.

"Well…yes, if you think me worthy, I will do it."

"Then Father Dominic will take you to the Scriptorium and advise you of the duties. You must on no account share this information with the other brothers, but we have a boy, who is under the abbey's protection, who will help you in your task. You will find him at the Grange mill, he can be trusted. His name is Robert the Mason."

CHAPTER 4

THE ERRAND BOY 1934

It was always the same. Whenever he finished his usual deliveries in town, Mr Woods said, "Do you fancy going up to Abbot's Wood, George?"

George's heart sank. He loathed the trail up to the big house, surrounded on all sides by overhanging trees and tangled undergrowth. Most of all he hated riding down the narrow lane past the abbey. It would be dusk by the time he got there and dark on the return journey. He knew Mr Woods was being kind, he always gave him an extra sixpence in his wages and there would be a three penny tip at the big house. George knew every penny mattered to his mother and tipped up all his wages, because he knew it helped to supplement his Dad's meagre railway porter's wage. He didn't mind, because his family was important and he knew how hard his Dad worked. He'd do anything for his Mam and Dad. But he sometimes wished they knew how hard it was to do his errands after school, especially this one.

At this time of year, the dark crept in silently and quickly, like a sneak thief. Autumn was a strange time, caught between the memory of long, sultry, summer and bright, bitter winter days. It somehow made things a little mysterious and frightening. This feeling doubled as soon as George reached the abbey.

"Right-o Mr Woods, I'll go now before it gets dark. What have I to take?" George asked, hiding the nervous tremor in his voice.

"Just the usual, son, joint o' beef, bacon hank and Waberthwaite sausages. Good luck the sausages come in today from Ravenglass, else they'd have had to have pork!" He wrapped the meat in paper as he was speaking.

George put on his bicycle clips again, did up his jacket and pulled his cap down over his ears. He walked out of the Butcher's shop, scuffing his clogs through the remnants of sawdust on the floor. He jumped down the two steps and on to the pavement. As he landed heavily, his steel tips sparked. He suddenly felt a bit braver, he was proud of his clogs. They made him different. They were not usually popular with school boys and most people wore boots or shoes in town, although George could name some kids who were so poor, they had no shoes. His clogs gave him a certain presence and he loved it when he could produce the blue sparks from the metal tips. He felt like he had power, a little bit of magic! He put the heavy package in the basket at the front of his bike, mounted and rode off.

There were a number of Victorian and Edwardian villas on the outskirts of Barrow and the long tree lined avenue of Abbey Road was fairly well lit by gas lamps. However, his resolve and bravery diminished by the time he reached Rating Lane. He was almost in the country now, the street lights became fewer and farther between, the traffic lessened and quietness descended. He whistled to keep his nerve, as he coasted round the corner into the lane past Manor Farm. The farm was not so bad, he could hear the cows and the clanking and hollering of the farm labourers and a warm orange glowed through the windows.

He peddled down the hill, rattling through the narrow opening between the remnants of the Western gateway. He shuddered as he flew past the 15th century cottage, it had a reputation for being haunted and it certainly lived up to it, in appearance. He travelled down to the bottom of the road, the abbey now visible. Its sandstone glowed pink in the final rays of the dying sun and rose up in front of him, powerful and majestic. The light was fading quickly now, he peddled standing up, to give him more power as he rode up the hill past the amphitheatre.

The trees leaned together over the road, branches touching and forming a natural tunnel. The boy rode on.

"Nearly there, just a bit longer and then home!" he said to himself, gritting his teeth.

He turned into the long drive to the big house, riding over the gravel, his wheels crunching and compressing the stones. Everything was in shadow and the night creatures were beginning to rouse. George could hear movements on either side of him and consoled himself that badgers and foxes would be stirring. He reached the big house and went straight round to the back door, where tradesmen were received.

He knocked on the door and waited. A woman in a black dress and snow white apron came to the door. She smiled, acknowledging the parcel he held.

"Thank you George, wait a minute, I'm sure there'll be something for you."

She turned and went in. As much as George wanted the customary tip, he wished that she would return quickly. It was really getting dark now and he had to go all the way back.

The maid returned. She pressed a silver sixpence into his cold hand. He looked at it and allowed himself to smile. "Cor! Thanks Miss." It was more than usual.

"It's because you are always so reliable and quick. Cook sent you this, too. Hope you enjoy it." She handed him a small package, wrapped in grease-proof paper. He peeped between the layers of paper and saw pieces of sticky, black treacle toffee.

"Ta, Miss. See you tomorrow!" he turned to leave.

He pushed the sixpence and the toffee deep into his coat pocket and got back on the bike. He peddled fast down the drive to the gate, ignoring the blanket of dark covering the wood. As he reached the gate, a figure walked swiftly across his path and into the bushes. He hadn't expected to see anyone and was taken aback. He skidded to a halt, gravel crunching and spattering across the drive. He looked into the bushes to see where the person had gone, but could see no sign.

George rode out into the lane. He reassured himself that his eyes were playing tricks, when, to his left he saw a shadowy figure. It was standing beside the old sandstone wall, which rose behind the abbey ruins, further down the hill. The figure, although featureless, was solid enough. George stood transfixed. He could not tell who it was, but he knew one thing, he had on something very long and hooded.

In fact, it almost looked like…

The realisation that the figure was a monk shocked him into action. His skin turned to goose-flesh and he was visibly shaking.

"Oh my God! Oh my God!" he muttered under his breath, "Why me? Why do I have to see a ghost?"

He clambered on to his bike again but stared fixedly at the figure which had not moved. He tried to tear his gaze away from the monk but failed. The figure turned to face him. Although George could not see his face, he knew the monk was looking at him. The monk raised an arm and turned his body towards the abbey and pointed. He then pointed at George and beckoned.

That was more than enough. Fascinated or not – he was off! He pedalled without looking back, skidding round corners and clipping the kerb stones. He didn't stop or turn back until he reached his back door. He pushed the bike into the yard and took off his clips and his cap. He stood for a moment, summoning up the memory of the monk. It scared him too much and he pushed the thought back down again. He turned and walked into the house.

CHAPTER 5

THE QUEST BEGINS

For the first time in weeks Rebecca felt excited and alive again. She didn't know why, but the strange events of recent days held promise and intrigue. They tried to read the book, but it hadn't helped much and so they had decided to go to the abbey instead. The sun was high in the sky and beat down ferociously. At one o' clock promptly, they met and set off up the lane.

They crossed the slow running trickle that had been the river and looked across the field. It was a long flat valley, bounded by a steep incline along its length. At the top of the hill was the lane which ran around the boundary of the abbey. They could see the old boundary wall, winding in and out of the trees like a rust coloured ribbon. There was a gatehouse, with black and white half-timbering, fronted by an immaculate topiary. At its side was the old gateway to a big house.

"I wonder who that is?" asked Danny, peering up towards the road.

Their gaze moved to where he was looking. A shadowy figure stood, motionless beside the sandstone wall. It was hard to make him out; his clothes blended in to the wall, obscured by the trees.

"He's watching us," said Megan, jumping to her

feet. She shielded her eyes against the sun, to try and get a better look.

"Who is it, then?" asked Danny, standing up.

They stood facing the road. The wall was higher than the road and further away. They gazed at the figure. Gradually, they edged closer, still keeping to the valley floor.

"He's got a long coat on! In this weather!" exclaimed Megan in disbelief.

Suddenly, the colour drained from Rebecca's face. The shock of recognition shuddered through her body. She stood as motionless as the figure and swallowed hard, feeling strangely cold on this hot, summer day.

"It's… it's a monk…" she whispered.

"What?" gasped Megan, "It's a … what?"

"A bloody monk!" hissed Danny.

They fell silent, unable to tear their eyes away from the mysterious spectre. The figure slowly turned and faced them, lifting an arm and pointing towards the abbey.

Then, as they watched, he disappeared. His disappearance was in the blink of an eye, not in a puff of smoke or a flash of light, just there one minute and then… gone!

They ran until they reached the museum steps and collapsed in a heap. Rebecca gasped for breath and Megan's heart pounded fast.

"What's this all about?" exclaimed Danny.

Rebecca flicked through the pages of the guide book for inspiration. It seemed hopeless, but she wanted to find a definite clue. A movement in the grounds caught her eye. They turned to look at what she had seen.

They knew instantly it was Mason and, with a common thought, leapt to their feet and ran down the gentle slope towards him.

"Where've ya been?" shouted Danny. They rushed over to meet him.

"Where did you go the other day?" asked Megan.

"Hold on! Slow down a bit! What's the rush?" he laughed as they reached him, "I set y' thinkin' a bit, did I?"

"Course you did! You gave us a little taste of a mystery and then *vanished!*" cried Danny.

"Oh I didn't disappear!" he said, "Just because you can't see a person...doesn't mean they're not there."

"How can you be there, if you're not there?" said Megan puzzled.

"Well, there are lots of things that we can't explain. There are things that we know are there, but we can't see – like electricity. You know, like gas..." Mason said smiling.

"Yeah, but that's not the same is it?" argued Danny, "That's science!"

"When this abbey was built, that would have been considered magic!" He turned away quietly.

"What are you saying? You used magic?" said Rebecca incredulously.

"There's magic... and there's *magic*."

This comment sounded very like what he had said about the treasure. It brought it back and provoked even more questions.

"What do you know about monks?" asked Megan.

Mason paused as though he was thinking hard

about his answer. "Well, what is it you want to *know* about monks?"

The children clamoured for answers. They wanted to know if Mason had seen the monk on the road. He raised his hands to his ears to block out the noise. He signalled them to calm down and be quiet.

"So," he whispered, "You've seen the brother then?"

"Yes! Just now, but who is he?" asked Rebecca impatiently.

"Oh you'll find out in time, when he wants to tell you who he is, he will…"

"But is he dead?" Danny demanded.

"Dead? Hmm! Well, he's not *alive* now… but *dead*? I'm not sure you could say that!"

"But you can't be alive and dead at the same time!" said Rebecca.

"Well… it depends I suppose… on what you mean. If you mean alive is a living, breathing creature – something that you can see and touch, then no he's not alive… but if you mean is he dead and gone from this world, then… no that's not right either."

Puzzled looks shot round the children's faces.

"I don't get it… what do you mean?" questioned Danny.

"Well… just because you can't see a person doesn't mean they are not there… and… just because you *can* see a person doesn't mean they *are* there!" Mason mused.

Danny shook his head in bewilderment. "But that's what you said before, about the magic thing. So do you mean the monk isn't a ghost of a dead person? He's real and he is somehow *here*, even though he isn't alive?"

"In a nutshell…" Mason smiled. "Time will tell… you will know *who* he is… *why* he wants you to see him… and what he wants you to do."

The children glanced quickly at each other. Mason smiled again.

"He wants us to do something?" questioned Danny. "How did he know we would be here?"

"Ah…" Mason mused, stroking his chin, thoughtfully, "Well, it's obvious; he's been waiting for you…"

"Waiting? What do you mean?" asked Rebecca.

"He needs you, to carry on where the boy left off… you've been chosen."

Danny erupted with a myriad of questions. Megan's face creased with frowns filled with confusion.

"Well, my friends, I'll have to be getting on. I've work to do…" said Mason.

Voices rose in protest, but Mason silenced them with a gesture. They all shut up, as if under a spell. The tall man turned and silently waved, as he strode off into the distance.

Rebecca stood, unable to move as she watched him disappear into the Cloister. When they discussed the strange afternoon they felt little wiser than before.

As they walked home, they weren't confident about walking past the gatehouse where they had seen the monk. Rebecca and Megan walked as close to the river as they could, not daring to look up the hill. Nobody spoke and they were conscious of their own breathing.

Rebecca was sure everyone could hear her heart beating. They walked down the narrow path, underneath the trees towards the 15th century packhorse bridge. Rebecca's breathing relaxed slightly as they crossed the bridge and pushed their way through the kissing gate, into the lane. They ran, faster until they reached the brow of the hill above their houses. They slowed down to a natural pace as they turned the corner into the close.

"We're on the edge of something really strange... something big... something that we've gotta do, but what it is I can't imagine..." announced Danny.

Megan shook her head solemnly. They fell quiet again. Rebecca broke the silence.

"Well, I think we will find out... soon. We need to keep our wits about us – there must be clues... we'll need to go back to the abbey again and this time we have to keep our heads and not be complete wusses if we see that monk!" she said with conviction.

Megan interjected, "Yeah, I think Becca's right, but I'm not keen on meeting him again – even if he isn't *dead* – whatever he is, he's not normal is he?"

Danny said, "Let's sleep on it and see what we can find out tomorrow. I'm going out with mum and dad, so I can't do nothin', can you?"

"Yes, I'll try, will you help, Megan?" asked Rebecca.

"O.K. but I'm a bit scared...do you think we should be dabbling in this?"

Rebecca shrugged, "I dunno... but we've got to try."

Chapter 6

Strange Creatures

After hours of turning and rolling, Rebecca pulled up her blind and pushed open the window as far as it would go. She took a deep breath, hoping that she would feel cooler. No chance! The air outside was as hot as that inside. She hung over the window sill, trying to find fresh air, looking out over the terraced garden, towards the railway line. In the distance she could make out the houses on the other side of the valley, some displaying lights, but most blacked out in darkness. The night was quiet and still, broken only by occasional weary bleats of the sheep pasturing in the fields.

As her eyes became accustomed to the dark she found she could see. The intense light emanating from the moon's silver disc, highlighted familiar features across the field and down the valley towards Park House Farm.

From the corner of her eye, she saw a flickering light. She turned, straining to see more clearly. The light grew in intensity. It was coming closer. She leaned further out of the window. Gasping, she saw the light swing to and fro. Light etched the outline of a long hooded robe. It didn't take too much brainwork to discover the figure was a monk. Rebecca was petrified and quickly bobbed down beneath the window sill.

Thoughts shot through her brain like a meteor shower. She steeled herself and slowly peeped over the sill. The window was open, but she could hear only the usual night noises. He was still there but had moved closer, just across the railway line, which ran along the bottom of the garden. He lifted the light; it was clearly an old lantern of some kind. Waving slowly, he looked straight at her. She froze, hardly daring to breathe, when from the left of the monk she saw another figure move. The slight, small figure moved unbelievably quickly and the lamp caught a gleam of metal in his hand. The monk turned, facing the other form. The figure jumped back, avoiding the monk. The monk raised his hand, the flat of his palm facing the creature. There was an unearthly howl and it fled. Rebecca had never seen anything like it before.

It was then that she spotted two more creatures, scattering and running wildly away from the monk. She could not identify the creatures, something about their appearance made her shudder. The monk turned again to face her. He moved seamlessly and smoothly. Calmness oozed from his very being. Gradually, Rebecca's apprehension melted, as she finally accepted that the monk was not a threat at all. In fact, it suddenly seemed that he was exactly the opposite. He was her guardian.

Danny and Megan had both been unable to sleep too. Danny lay still, staring up at the ceiling, wondering when he would manage to drop off to sleep. Soft moonlight shadows flickered and changed the ceiling. He could make out the silhouette of leaves and branches from the tree outside his bedroom window. The silvery light filtered gently into the room. Images played along the wall, he felt relaxed and soothed. His eye lids closed momentarily. When he opened them again, the shadow had changed.

The lacy pattern of the leaves distorted and closed up. Danny caught his breath. The image became a monkey like creature, odd and thin. He was terrified, unable to move or breathe. The shadow moved along the outline of one of the branches. It looked scarily close. When he could stand it no longer, Danny sat up in bed, scrambled to the window and peered into the tree, which in reality, was not close at all. He made out the shape of the branches and within it he could see the creature. It was angular and bony, human but not human, strange and frightening. Danny pulled away from the window and hid behind the wall. He peeped round the window frame and he could still see it.

Something rustled in the bushes below. He saw to his horror that there was another one in the garden. He prayed quietly that they wouldn't hear his heart pounding against his rib-cage. He looked over to Megan's house on the other side of the close and saw two more of the things in her garden. They were running around the flower beds like rodents. Danny wondered if Megan was aware of these strange animals patrolling her garden.

His answer came quickly. A piercing scream echoed across the street, from the direction of number

22. The creatures stopped, looked sharply round and then started to move again. Suddenly, the creatures froze and looked towards the corner of the road. A white mist appeared, illuminated by the street light on the other side of the street, along from Rebecca's house. A commotion was going on at Megan's house, lights snapping on and people moving, but Danny was transfixed by the mist. A figure was forming within its centre, becoming denser and clearer. It was the monk.

The creatures scattered in different directions, away from the monk. He stood firmly and watched them until they had all disappeared into the night. Danny sighed with relief and felt that his earlier fear of the monk had evaporated and he knew that he was on their side. The monk remained still for a second and then he looked directly at Danny and raised a hand to wave. Danny was so astonished that he waved back. With that the monk turned, the mist enveloping him and finally melting away to nothing but a whisper.

Next day, they met at Megan's, each desperate to tell their experiences of the night before.

"They were dead scary weren't they? They looked like something out of a horror film or something; creepy, ugly, weird looking things," said Megan, "I screamed my head off and mum and dad had to come in and cuddle me. I hope I never see them again, you don't think we will, do you?"

She shuddered and pulled a face as though she had just taken a dose of particularly disgusting medicine.

"I went cold when I saw "them", I couldn't tell

what they were, but they didn't half move fast. I saw that flippin' monk as well – but, d'ya know, I wasn't scared of him this time!" Danny paused as if convincing himself, "At least… I don't think I was."

"It's strange – neither was I" exclaimed Rebecca, "But I didn't like the *things*, they were eerie… and they remind me of something, but I don't know what."

"Yes, I thought they must be an animal or something.…" Danny added.

"I don't fancy coming across them again, but perhaps we should tell Mason about it," began Rebecca.

Danny groaned.

"But that means going down to the abbey again…" his voice tapered off.

It took them a little time to decide what to do. They wanted to find out about the quest, but it was hard to put the night's events out of their minds. They returned to the abbey the next day, albeit apprehensively. This time as they crossed the field a part of Rebecca secretly hoped the monk would re-appear – he was something of a saviour after the incident with the night creatures.

They reached the abbey ruins without any strange occurrences. They saw Mason in the area of the old infirmary, repairing a low wall. They shouted to him over the metal railings. He looked up and smiled, beckoning them to come in. They ran around the perimeter of the abbey and up the steps to the museum entrance. They paid and went through the museum and into the abbey grounds.

"We're gonna own this abbey soon, if we keep having to pay like this!" exclaimed Danny.

"You won't be complaining if we find the treasure," retorted Megan.

"It depends what the treasure is… it might not be gold or silver or jewels you know…" suggested Rebecca.

The children ran through the cemetery and along the reredorter until they reached the buttery – the only part of the abbey with a roof. Footsteps echoed as they ran across the uneven cobbled floor and out into the infirmary. Mason was awaiting their approach.

Suddenly, a raucous cackle crackled through the air. Four sleek magpies swooped, furiously flapping black, tattered wings, blue and white gleaming in the sunlight. They flew perilously close and the swish of wings hissed in the children's ears.

"They're coming straight for us!" shrieked Megan.

They sprinted as fast as they could, protecting their heads with their hands. Suddenly, the pitch of the birds' cries rose in panic. A booming voice drowned out the screeching. Mason scattered them, flailing long arms and trowel in a circular fashion, like a human windmill. The magpies flapped ferociously, gaining height and circling menacingly, finally flying into the trees in Abbot's Wood.

The children dropped to the grass catching their breath and trembling. Mason sank to the ground, removing his hard hat and mopping his forehead with his handkerchief.

"Well," he said, shaking his head, "That's a turn up…"

Danny asked, "What is?"

"The old magpies… Someone's bothered about you lot!"

Mason slowly replaced his helmet. He stroked his chin, thoughtfully, a gesture they were now familiar with.

"It's begun; I think you need to know a few things."

The children looked attentively at him, waiting for him to start.

"You've attracted attention", they all opened their mouths to speak, their minds full of questions. Mason gestured them to wait.

"You need to be prepared. The treasure has been hidden since old Henry's time… and its time it was found and made safe for good. They want it so badly and it's a wicked time… they could just manage it! The treasure must be safe and it must be given to those who can take care of it. It holds great power and in the wrong hands, well…" the words hung in the air like a black cloud. Mason will help, Masons have always helped. The boy came close… he helped to keep it hidden… he'll help again… you'll see him, he will come to you."

"Well, that's really cleared that up, Mr Mason!" said Danny.

"Time will tell, young lad… time will tell! You must search, but *they* won't like you looking. The treasure is still within the abbey lands and *they* are coming closer to it all the time. We… *you* have got to save it!"

"But where do we start? What *is* the treasure?" asked Danny.

"You need to discover that yourself, but remember

who owned it and what it stood for, before you go off looking for gold and jewels. It's abbey treasure, not a pirate hoard."

"What about "them"... are they bad or something?" asked Megan.

"Bad and *very* dangerous!" whispered Mason in hushed tones.

"Something strange happened to us last night," interrupted Rebecca.

Mason raised his eyebrows and looked sharply at her. She continued slowly.

"There were weird creatures... and the monk... at our houses."

Mason's face creased into worried lines, "What creatures? The magpies?"

"No, not them...skinny, bony monkey things," she added.

"Ah... I might have known. Don't worry; they can only use them at night... they are creatures of the dark."

"Is that supposed to make us feel better? Cos it don't," remarked Danny. "What are they anyway?"

"You can find them... they're all around the abbey... look carefully. The brother... well, he is around too. He doesn't stray far from the abbey... you can find him if you look."

"Did he hide the treasure?" asked Rebecca excitedly.

"He was its guardian and he passed his knowledge onto others to protect it."

"But what are we supposed to do?" she exclaimed, exasperated.

"Start with the swan... think hard about it!" he

answered. "The treasure will reveal itself. He looked after it, saving it for the future, passing it on to the next guardian. When Henry got rid of the abbey, others thought they could take it. By destroying the abbey he let them in."

"You said something about a boy… what's that all about?" asked Danny.

"The boy helped. He'll help again; watch out for him and…"

Mason's eyes tracked along the cloister wall, a man was walking down the steps and onto the path. He stood up and turned away. "Well, I'm off now, but be careful and stay alert. I can guide, but it's your quest… not mine!" With that he strode off to where he had been working, picked up his bucket and tool bag and walked away, leaving the children astounded by his abrupt exit.

They had no time to discuss the odd conversation, because the man who had been walking through the cloister was now walking purposefully towards them. He was a thin, tall, balding man, who seemed to glide across the grass, he walked so quickly. He was dressed smartly in a dark suit, with a crisp white shirt and shiny black tie. He reminded Rebecca of an undertaker, but his eyes were made of flint. He smiled at them, a cold smile which stayed on his lips, not travelling to his eyes as a smile should.

"I hope you have your tickets with you. Too many youngsters have been climbing over the railings to get in!" he held out a long, thin hand to receive evidence of their entry ticket.

"Course we've paid!" Danny said in a disgusted tone.

"I would like to see please," he said, undeterred.

They searched in pockets and purses, each finding a crumpled green ticket and showing him. He looked disgruntled that they could prove their honesty.

"Good," he said, his expression disappointed, "But I will be particularly watching you… we have suffered from a lot of vandalism recently."

"We wouldn't do anything like that!" protested Rebecca.

"I don't trust children and I *will* be watching for you. I am Mr Steele and I know everything that goes on in this abbey. What are you trying to find here? You seem to have visited the abbey rather frequently recently, so the cashier tells me?" he enquired.

"We're looking for t…" began Megan.

"… tiles and carvings," interjected Danny quickly. Something told him this man was not someone to share their quest with. "We've got a school project to do."

"Hmmm. I see, well, as I said, I will be watching you." With that, he turned on his heel and returned the way he came.

As soon as he had gone Megan thumped Danny. "What did you lie for?"

"Because you great plonker, we don't want everyone knowing about our quest. We don't know who "they" are, do we?"

"I never thought…" replied Megan, looking crestfallen.

"Don't worry Megan," said Rebecca, glaring at

Danny. She smiled kindly at her and the girl returned it gratefully.

"Let's go and look at the swan grave and the museum again and see if we can find some clues this time," Danny added.

"Yeah but not now, while he's still lurking," said Rebecca indicating the man, who was standing on the top step in front of the nave of the church, looking in their direction. They moved away from Mr Steele and walked home through the lane in silence.

That night, although they were all nervous about a return of the strange creatures, they were so tired that they fell asleep straight away. The night passed peacefully, or so they believed...

Chapter 7

The secret

George had discovered a most important clue and knew it was precious. He had been too nervous to search for the next one alone and had taken his best mate Sid with him for moral support. Sid wasn't clear about what they were doing, but was happy to go along for the ride. The two of them left their bikes near the Old Custom House.

They reached the little jetty at the end of Roa Island to wait for the ferryman. The two lads sat down, dangling their legs over the side of the wooden jetty. Sid pulled out a small packet. He carefully unwrapped the folded greaseproof paper and revealed two buns, filled with fresh, crumbly Lancashire cheese; George's favourite. Sid handed one to George and the boys tucked into them with relish. As they finished, the small rowing boat approached, gliding smoothly across the calm sea, the waves from the oars lapping softly and rippling the surface of the water.

The boys waited for the boat to dock. The red haired ferryman flashed a toothless smile at them and said, "You wantin' to go over t' Piel then?"

They nodded and climbed into the little boat. The man held out his hand for payment and the boys handed over their threepence. The journey was short; Piel Island was a small island just off the Furness coast. It was less than two miles across and at any point its beaches were visible. It was largely uninhabited, apart from a few sheep and a small row of cottages and oddly, a pub!

However, its claim to fame was the 13th century castle which dominated the island. It had fallen into disrepair long ago, but it had once played a part in English history. George loved history and knew all about it. The castle belonged to the abbey and had been built to provide protection from the rampaging Scots.

Its major piece in the history jigsaw was when young Lambert Simnel, a pretender to the throne, had landed with an army and marched on London. It had all ended in tears of course, but it sort of put Furness on the historical map. For George, this added to the magic of the place. The boatman threw the rope over the end of the little pier and steadied the boat with his oar. The boys jumped out and the ferryman reminded them to be ready at four to make the trip back to the mainland.

The boys walked up the beach towards the castle. It loomed large above them, crumbling, but still powerful. They scrambled up the banking and climbed over the foundations of the outer walls. Once in the inner bailey of the castle, George stopped and looked around him, finding his bearings. He pulled a small piece of paper from his pocket and smoothed it out. Sid looked over his shoulder, peering at the strange writing on the paper. It showed a rough drawing of the island and a rudimentary plan of the castle and its keep.

"Blimey, Georgie! Where did you get that from?" he asked. "Is it what the castle used to be like?"

"Yes! It hasn't changed much… but some stonework has collapsed."

They looked around and together tried to orientate the map. They looked up at the remains of the keep and then the curtain walls around the outside. In a split second George was running off towards the highest point of the castle. Sid followed and they stopped at the arch. George looked at the map again and began to read the script on the paper.

"Step onwards to ye place of fforgetting… within ye shall find that which ye seeke… a remembrance of the holy man… sacred… his bones carried cross ye sands for refuge… heathens…"

"That's as clear as mud… i'nt it?" Sid sighed.

"It's a clue, don't you see? It's telling us where to look… where to go next."

"Alright, clever clogs! What's a place of forgetting, when it's at home?"

George looked at him blankly. "I haven't a clue! Let's go and explore."

They went into the base of the pele tower and stepped carefully over the nettles and brambles. As they moved forward the weeds got thicker, it looked as though nobody had ventured in for years! George picked up a stick and thrashed at the undergrowth, beating down some of the weeds. They walked around observing everything closely, hoping for a clue or a direction. Suddenly, Sid gave a yell and disappeared into the grass. Small flies and butterflies flew up from where he had vanished and George heard him swear.

"Damn and blast it!"

George knew it must be serious, Sid never swore, he was too aware of the back of his mother's hand across his legs... but whatever had happened, made him forget the usual rules.

George found his friend nursing a pair of bloodied knees and prickled hands. He had tripped over rubble and what looked like a drain grid.

"You alright, mate?" he asked with concern.

"Yeah, 'suppose so... didn't see this flaming grid."

As George helped him to his feet, they both looked down at the cause of the accident. George began pulling the grass and weeds away from the drain. He revealed a much larger grid than he had at first realised. He became excited and frantically pulled away the vegetation more fiercely.

"I know what it is! I know! It's an oubliette!! You know – we did it in history! They chucked people down and left 'em... to die!"

"Er, suppose so, wasn't it French or summat?"

"Yes. That's right, but what monks would want it for I don't know!"

"Well, p'raps it wasn't used for prisoners, maybe they stored stuff down there", suggested Sid, "or maybe it was for them monks who was bad?"

George lay down on the grass on his stomach and peered down into the hole. He reached down with his hands and felt around the edge of the hole, shuffling along as he did so. He had barely moved along the second side when he stopped and called out.

"Hey! There's something here on the ledge... its

wrapped in cloth or something…" he stretched out and forced his arm further down through the grating, wincing and straining as he reached into the hole. He struggled to free the package and gave an almighty tug, finally dragging it free placing it on the grass in front of him.

Sid crouched down beside his friend and waited with anticipation. The little packet was wrapped in leather and bound with a rough twine, which was beginning to fray. He took out a small penknife, which he always carried with him and cut the binding. He carefully unfolded the piece of old leather and revealed a strange, small carving. It was no bigger than his palm and he gazed thoughtfully at it. It was made from a soft limestone and the detail on it was amazing.

The little figure was a man in long robes. His hand was raised in front of his chest and a cross shape was carved the full length of his robe. He had a tall hat, again marked with a cross. George turned it over and inspected the back of the figure. On the back there was a tiny but perfect carving of a swan.

"It looks like a bishop to me, Sid."

"How can you tell?"

"It's the cross and the hat; it reminds me of a bishop's hat. Maybe it's an abbot. After all, this place belonged to the monks."

Sid looked thoughtful, "Hmm, but it isn't made from the same stone is it? Isn't this place the same as the abbey – sandstone? That little man is made out of white stone…" he trailed off, looking a bit embarrassed at saying so much.

"Sid! You're brilliant!"

Sid looked puzzled. If he was brilliant, he didn't actually know why or how!

"Well, it's not come from here *or* the abbey has it? Not if it's different stone. Where can it be from? It's sort of rough on the base... like it's been broken off or something."

"So, what are we going to do, then? How can we find out where it's from?"

"I'm not sure, but I'm going to ask dad, he might have some ideas about the stone... or I could take it to me Granddad's, he *would* know, he's a builder and works with stone all the time... and he's shown me special stones he's found on the fells and in the dry stone walls, when he's repairing them. Some of them are as old as the hills themselves."

"How we gonna find out who he is then?"

"We'll go down the library... we can look it up in some of the books down there!" said George, undaunted by Sid's look of dismay.

The boys started to walk down towards the beach. They caught sight of the little rowing boat making its way across the narrow channel, towards the jetty. The boys ran to the water's edge and jumped up and down shouting, pretending to be castaways, about to be rescued.

The ferryman was visible on the mainland. He was talking to someone standing on the jetty. The tall, thin man pointed to the island. The boys stopped their game of castaways and stood watching. Something about him made their hair stand on end. He stared right at them, in fact it seemed as though his eyes were drilling into them and rooting out all their secrets. George wanted to run and hide, but there was nowhere to go. They were captives on the island until the ferry reached them.

The man got into the little boat and sat perfectly still, perched like a bird of prey, facing them. George quickly stuffed the little figure into his shirt front and pulled his sweater over it. He didn't know why, but this man was a threat and the discovery must be protected at all costs.

The boat arrived and the boys waited for the man to get out. He remained seated and his cold eyes bored into them.

"Jump in lads," said the boatman, "This fella's just out fer t' ride."

George's heart fluttered. He and Sid exchanged glances. The man smiled an unpleasant smile. The effect was disturbing and Sid swallowed hard.

"How nice of you to join us. What have you been up to on the island today?" he enquired with a sinister politeness.

George was speechless for a second but Sid saved the day.

"Nowt Mister! Just over for a picnic that's all… nowt much t' see really."

The man did not look convinced and continued to stare intensely.

The short journey lasted forever, but finally the boat drew close to the jetty. In a flash George grabbed Sid's arm and dragged him to his feet, wobbling the little boat. The strange man clutched the side of the boat and the ferryman tried to steady it with the oar.

Sid and George leapt onto the jetty and ran off towards their bikes. The ferryman shouted at them as they sent the boat rocking and the man almost lost his balance. They didn't stop until they reached their bikes and then peddled relentlessly, until they skidded into Manchester Street.

The next thing Rebecca knew was her lovely, smiling, twinkly eyed Granddad had gone. She couldn't bring herself to say "died"; because that wasn't a word she could connect with Granddad. He had been her best friend always, she couldn't imagine being without him for the rest of her life.

She sat by the river, alone, dangling her legs over the edge of the bridge; she could almost imagine him walking along the tree lined path with his walking stick. She could sense his closeness under the trees, dappled by the warm sunlight. She soaked up the warmth of the sun and closed her eyes, the lids heavy and drowsy. For a moment she was safe, like she was when she sat in his old armchair, cosy in his warm embrace when he was still here.

Unexpectedly, her mood changed. The back of her neck tingled and her stomach lurched. A shiver rippled its way down her spine and made her tremble. Something was going to happen. The same feeling of dread and foreboding that she had had during the thunderstorm returned. Across the field she could see a tall, thin man looking at her. Granddad's voice whispered in her ear, "Run, Rebecca, run and hide… I'll be here to look after you…"

She knew he was still with her even if he was inside her head.

CHAPTER 8

THE STONE

George padded along the lane towards Roose village, only pausing briefly to look behind. The day was sultry and airless, making it difficult to run. The rubber soles of his plimsolls hardly touched the surface of the road. George's face was red and moist with sweat and his chest felt as though it would burst.

He reached the old railway bridge at the top of the lane, where he could survey the valley past the farm towards Bow Bridge. He bent over with his hands on his knees, gasping for breath and trying to think. The parchment was in his shorts pocket and he could feel it crinkling against his thigh. He stood up and looked around quickly, like a hunted animal. He was relieved that he could see nothing unusual.

George steadied himself and turned to walk to Roose. He walked across Boulton's Common and paused again to look behind. Gradually as he walked down the hill, he relaxed, feeling a little safer. He approached the new, semi-detached houses in Red River Road. Some were fully built and looked ready to be lived in, but some were still under construction. He sauntered down the road, looking at the smart homes, and could not help but compare them to his own small terraced house in the town. They seemed large and had a front and back garden. Mam and Dad's house had a yard and the front door opened straight onto the street. One day he'd have a house like that, he thought.

He paused to look at one house. Someone was about to move in. There was newspaper at the windows and the flowerbeds had been planted around the small, neat lawn with shrubs and a hedge. It looked a nice house, one that he would be proud to live in, he thought. His gaze fell on a chunk of sandstone beneath the front window, in front of the house. He looked around to check that the coast was clear and walked up the gravel drive. He couldn't resist examining it. George knelt down and touched the sandstone.

He was surprised to discover that it was not a stone; it had clearly been carved from a single block of sandstone and had a cavity in the centre. He looked closely and tried to work out what it was used for. It looked like a strange sink. He pulled it away from the wall and examined it further. On the front panel was a faint carving of a swan. He traced the outline with a grubby finger; he knew instinctively this was where to leave his clue, in case he needed to remind himself… or someone else in the future?

Underneath was flat, but in the centre there was a small dint of about four inches in depth. George peered into it and poked inside it with his finger, it was dry and clean. He had a sudden brainwave. The parchment would fit inside perfectly. He needed to keep it dry and thought for a second. Slowly he took out a neatly folded piece of tin foil from his pocket.

George carefully unfolded the tin foil and smoothed it out. He took the parchment out and laid it on top of the foil. He cautiously rolled it into a small tube. He reached into his pocket for a piece of string. He took his penknife and cut it and tied it gently around the roll. Pleased with his work, he then inserted it into the space beneath the stone. It fitted well and he pushed it as far into it as he could, without damaging it. He then looked around for something to plug the opening with. He rummaged in the flowerbed to find stones and rocks which might fit. After a lot of rooting about he grasped a small piece of red house brick. He managed to force it in. He then tipped up the block and slid it back to its original position. He stood up, pleased with his efforts. He had a pleasant glow inside and knew the parchment would be safe for the time being. He planned to return when it was safe but little did he know it would be a long time before he was able… and through no fault of his own.

That night George tossed and turned in bed. His earlier feeling of relief and safety evaporated with a torrent of dreams and nightmares. He grew hotter and hotter and was sick to his stomach. He drifted in and out of sleep and existed in a world between nightmare and reality. He jumped and woke up from his uneasy rest. Shivering and clammy and his head pounding, he climbed from the bed he shared with his older brother, Billy. The sheets were crumpled and damp with sweat. Billy grunted and turned over.

George had to get to the small attic window to get some air. He climbed up onto the oak chest and reached up to the window to push it open. The cool air passed over his face and for a moment he felt better. He looked out into the night sky and could see the stars and the bright full moon. The night was peaceful, apart from the barking of a dog in the distance. George was soothed and took a deep breath, closing his eyes.

He opened them immediately, hearing a scrambling noise on the slate roof. Stretching up, he peered over the edge of the window frame. Something was moving, he reckoned it was a cat, it moved quickly. The roof was clear. Yes, it was a cat, he was sure.

Suddenly, he jumped back, almost falling backwards off the chest. He couldn't help but cry out. A hideous monkey like creature scuttled across the roof tiles close to the window. Its face was gaunt and ugly, with large pointed ears framing it. Angular limbs jutted out and sprang like powerful levers as the creature moved. It turned to look directly at him and its scowling face hardened as it caught him in its view. Small red eyes bored into his very soul. It was searching for something and he felt it could read his mind. He panicked and stumbled in his haste to get away. With an almighty crash he slipped off the chest and knocked the enamel wash bowl and jug flying across the room, spilling water over the bed.

Suddenly, noise and commotion chased away the family's sleep. Billy shouted with shock as the water soaked the back of his nightshirt and George crashed to the floor at the same time as the jug and bowl rattled to the floor. As George lay sweating and shivering on the attic floor he could see the creature peering at him through the sky light, which slammed shut as George had fallen. He couldn't contain his fear and screamed at the top of his voice.

His mother and father ran up the stairs to the attic room the boys shared.

"What on earth is happening?" demanded his mother.

"It's our Titch, Mam! He's gone mad!" offered Bill. "He soaked me through and then fell on the floor screaming like a girl. He's gone mad!"

They all turned to look at George, or Titch as the family had nicknamed him.

He was still shivering and beads of sweat glistened on his reddened face.

"Titch! Has't tha gone daft, lad?" said his Dad in his broad Cumberland accent.

There was no answer. Titch was asleep. Titch was unconscious.

The fever and the headaches lasted for a fortnight. With them came the "hallucinations", as his Gran called them. George had meningitis which in 1934, with no antibiotics, was nearly always fatal. His Gran sat with him throughout the terrible illness. He thrashed about, desperately screaming about the terrifying creatures he saw; she wiped his hot brow with a damp cloth, trying to soothe away the nightmares. She could never see them. In fact, at first, it took some persuasion to convince her George's illness wasn't a result of smoking! His mother and Gran sat with him for long hours, nursing him, both their faces etched with worry.

The boy was delirious. He slept fitfully, talking in

his sleep, flailing about and staring glassy eyed, recognising nobody. On a number of occasions he screamed out and tried to climb away from whatever monsters were persecuting him. He pointed feverishly at the sky light and later on at the window in the front room where they had quarantined him. The creatures would not leave him in peace. They knew he had discovered something and they wanted it. He was terrified, but he could not make his mother see sense and listen to him. They held him down and tried to soothe him, but he could still see the creatures. They mopped his forehead with a damp flannel and tried desperately to soothe his nightmares.

George heard the doctor say that he was fighting for his life. They said the creatures he was seeing were not real at all. He knew he *was* ill, but he knew the creatures *were* real.

Eventually, after weeks of crushing headaches, fever, vomiting and night terrors, George came through. His mother had nursed him carefully, trusting to instinct and common sense. She had ignored the suggestion from the doctor to allow a surgeon to operate on his head and merely waited.

When he did begin to recover, the illness left him with terrible headaches and a dreadful weakness. His mother arranged for him to stay with Auntie Annie and Uncle Joe in New Southgate, in London, so that he could attend a clinic at the Royal Northern Hospital. He did not know then, that the kindly Spanish Doctor Zamora who was treating him was using new methods to return him to full health. The foul smelling ointment he had to stick up his nose was actually life saving antibiotics. It was going to be a long recovery. Worse still, he forgot things and as the weeks passed, he had erased many details of the quest from his memory. It would be years before the memories would begin to re-emerge... and then it would be too late.

CHAPTER 9

SEEKING

It was drizzling and muggy. The clouds were heavy, leaden grey. Rebecca hated summer days like this, they seemed miserable and boring. Worse still, they made her think of Granddad. She pulled up the blind in her room and sighed, looking out over the garden to the fields opposite. The sheep were scattered like cotton wool across the grass. Following the path of a little pied-wagtail as it flew swiftly from tree to tree, she gasped in astonishment as she suddenly caught sight of the circular paved patio. Mum's tubs and planters had all been upturned and the plants scattered across the gravel. Two were broken and Rebecca could see footprints all over the rockery beds.

She ran downstairs to tell Mum and Dad. They already knew and had been very cross.

"It's a cat or a stray dog I expect! What a mess!" said Mum, dismayed.

"Well, it was fine when Sam went out last night," replied Dad. Sam was their chocolate brown Labrador, named after Granddad.

"You're sure he couldn't have done it?" suggested Mum.

"No, I don't think so!"

Rebecca knew in her heart it was not Sam at all. She had a sneaking feeling that she knew exactly what had done it. However, she wasn't about to explain the strange things to her parents. It made her shudder to think that they had been trampling the garden when she was asleep last night. She wondered what they were looking for.

After breakfast she went into the garden to investigate. The footmarks were peculiar. They were trefoil shaped, with three pointed toes *and* they were surprisingly large. The earth had been scraped and scuffed and amongst the footprints there was a residue of sandstone flakes and dust. She was puzzled about where it had come from, the nearest sandstone lay at the abbey. Sam came out too, sniffing and digging with his large front paws, trying to help. He seemed unsettled and Rebecca was surprised that he hadn't barked last night. The dog ran to and fro sniffing for whomever, or whatever had committed this piece of vandalism. He growled deep in his throat and curled back his lip.

"What's up, lad?" she said, "Can you smell them?"

She went to call for the others. Megan was out with her parents for the day, which was disappointing but, undeterred she went to call for Danny. He was in. He came bounding out like an excited puppy.

"You won't believe it – someone's been in our back garden and trashed the pots and the tubs. Mam's gone spare! She's only just done them and they cost a packet!"

"Same happened to us Danny! All the planters smashed and tipped out and whopping footprints all over the show!" replied Rebecca.

"What do you think they were after? It's gotta be them monkey things again ain't it?" said Danny.

They ran across the cul-de-sac towards Megan's house, the gate was swinging open. They stole a look into the garden. The same devastation met their eyes. The pots, hanging baskets and the compost bin were upturned and disturbed.

"Wha' da they think we've got?" asked Danny.

"I don't know, but whatever it is, it must be important. They obviously think we've found something. Perhaps we *should* have found something."

Rebecca's dad shouted her. He asked them to go to Grandma's house to fetch spare pots to replant some of the herbs and flowers. They waited on the doorstep for her to answer the door. Suddenly, something caught Rebecca's eye. Beneath the bay window, there was a block of sandstone. She had seen it a dozen times before and had never really looked at it properly.

Rebecca jumped off the step and pulled Danny down to kneel in front of the stone. She traced the carving with her finger, brushing away some of the moss which covered the grooves. It revealed a faint outline of a swan.

"It's a sign! It's a sign!" she cried excitedly.

"Wow! I can't believe it. Here at your Gran's all the time."

They pulled it away from the wall, where it had been for years. They inspected it closely. Nothing of remark was seen, but then, with some difficulty they turned the stone upside down. The base was not smooth. Danny poked at the base with his finger. A piece of brick had been jammed into the aperture. They both tried to pull it out, but it was fixed hard. Danny picked up a stick and tried to lever the stone from it. Eventually, the stone popped out and bounced onto the path.

Danny felt inside the hole.

"I think there's something in here!" he was excitedly peering into it and trying to pull out whatever was in there. After a little bit of manipulation a small roll of foil came out. It lay there for a moment as the children gazed, incredulous. Rebecca gently picked it up and carefully unrolled it. The foil had stuck to the back of the parchment; she flattened it and looked at the faint writing on the yellowed parchment.

She could not make out the script easily, but there was a small map drawn on it. Suddenly, she felt cold and shivers rippled down her back. Quickly, she clasped it close to her chest and took in a sharp breath.

"Let's go in, we'll get something to put it in," she said, whispering.

Grandma was pleased to see them and offered them a drink and a biscuit. Rebecca went into her cupboard; she rooted through the array of out grown toys, until she found what she was looking for. She pulled out a small plastic wallet and opened it.

"We'll put it in here, it'll be safe and it won't be noticed!"

"Noticed by who?" asked Danny, puzzled.

"You don't know who's about... look at what happened last night," replied Rebecca.

Danny paused and then nodded his head.

"We've got to find Mason I think...we may have what they were after last night!" she said, seriously.

Again Danny nodded.

The two slipped quietly into the street. The weather was still overcast and heavy. They were jumpy and walked quickly up the hill towards their street. Rebecca imagined eyes peering at them from every window and that something was hiding in every bush. They were thankful to reach home in one piece.

"How are we going to get to the abbey to talk to Mason and show him the manuscript?" asked Danny.

"I dunno..." Rebecca answered.

Both children wondered if they could risk going to the abbey alone. As they thought about their predicament their attention was attracted by a series of movements to their side and behind them. Silently two huge blue streaked magpies swooped into the boughs of the tree, another pair perched on the top of the honeysuckle covered fence and as they watched three more circled ominously in the air above the decking.

"Seven!! Seven magpies... seven for a secret never to be told...!" squealed Rebecca hysterically, quoting from the old rhyme.

Danny sensed the panic in her voice and he quickly grabbed her hand and pulled her up the meandering path to the house. As he did so, the birds slowly flapped their large wings and began to rise into the air, circling the garden like vultures.

They retreated into the kitchen. Rebecca's mum turned around and smiled at them.

"I suppose you two want some lunch?" she asked.

She didn't wait for an answer, but proceeded to make sandwiches. She continued to talk, oblivious of their anxiety.

"After lunch I thought I'd take you out somewhere– it is the holidays after all. Where would you like to go?"

The children looked at each other briefly and both said in unison,

"The abbey!"

"The abbey? But you've been there so many times; wouldn't you like to go somewhere different?"

The pair shook their heads and Rebecca's mum shrugged and agreed to take them.

The children felt braver going to the abbey with an adult, despite the fact that she didn't know that she was their unofficial bodyguard. They followed her into the museum and waited until she had paid. They tried to avoid the cashier's gaze, as they didn't want her telling Mum how often they came.

They wandered around the museum with Mum, listening politely as she pointed things out to them. Around the corner they stopped in front of a carving. They read the label beneath. It said that the carving was from the top of a capital of a column and showed *strange monkey-like creatures, whose origin is unknown.* Rebecca whispered "They look like those things we saw in the garden… but they can't be, they're made of stone…"

Danny nodded.

"It's weird, but we did see chips of sandstone on the floor…"

They stopped talking and followed Rebecca's mum into the abbey grounds.

In the distance Mr Mason was working on the foundations. Rebecca's eyes widened in surprise as her mum briskly walked across the grass towards Mr Mason. He looked up and smiled. She returned the smile and said hello.

"I was sorry to hear about your dad... I've known him a long time, very sad."

The children stared at each other in amazement. How did he know Granddad?

"We've got to try and talk to him on our own... how are we going to do that, now?" hissed Rebecca.

"It's difficult... can we get your mum away from him... or away from us, so we can tell him?"

Danny looked glum. The trip would be wasted if they were unable to talk to Mason. Mason pointed back up to the museum and nodded. Mum turned to them and said, "I'm just going up to the shop, apparently there's a new book about the abbey, so I thought I'd get it and sit over there and have a read, while you two explore... if you would like to?"

The children jumped at the suggestion, amazed at their luck. Mum turned and walked off towards the museum, waving her hand casually as she left.

"Wow! That was a lucky break!" said Danny," It's almost as if she knew we needed to talk to Mason."

"Yeah! Like magic – almost..." muttered Rebecca.

Soon, they were talking together in hushed voices. Mason frowned and his expression became very serious.

"This is becoming dangerous, you must be wary. They know you've found something…"

"But we only found it today… they can't have known we *would* find it… can they?" said Rebecca.

"You would be surprised…"

"You have a clue – the boy saw to that. The quest was taken out of his hands… but it can be won, this time."

"Who is the boy? You mentioned him before… " asked Danny.

"He will find you when it's time."

Rebecca took out the wallet and carefully pulled out the paper. She smoothed it out gently and everyone gathered around to look closely at it.

"I think the parchment is old, but some of the writing isn't quite as old. Look! It looks like it's been torn from a book… but the writing is in faint pencil."

Mason smiled at her and nodded.

"So why would someone write on old paper in pencil?" asked Danny.

"Maybe they couldn't find anything else to write on?"

They examined the faint script, the pencil marks appearing almost violet they were so faded. It was difficult to see and they held it up to the light. The words looked clearer and they were able to decipher some of them.

"On Rabbit Hill… find… in the light…" read Rebecca, "Oswald's friend… key. The swan is his… his place… What does it mean?"

Mr Mason stood up and picked up his trowel.

"Clues, I expect, but keep it safe and try to avoid *them*."

They could make little sense of the small map, although some familiar places were visible, but it was unclear what it was showing. Mason walked away, pausing to talk to Rebecca's mum, who was walking back towards them. Rebecca began to fold the paper and put it into the little folder. A number of magpies silently landed one by one on top of the infirmary walls. She hastily pushed the wallet into her jeans pocket and stood up. She nodded at the birds to Danny. He jumped up and began to shoo them away.

The birds rose in a cloud of black and blue and slowly circled the children. As they walked away from the sinister birds, they flew closer, swooping silently around them. The children panicked and started to run, provoking them into a more direct attack. Rebecca screamed and Danny tried to hit at the birds with his hands. The children kept running and as they did so, Mason strode up, waving his trowel and hard hat at the birds. Rebecca's mum stood helpless, watching as Mason extricated the frightened children from the magpies. Mason towered powerfully above the children. He was silhouetted against the sun, tall and supreme. He raised his hand and called a string of words, which were unrecognisable to the children. Rebecca had seen this gesture before, but could not place where.

"Oh are you alright? Those terrible birds... did they hurt you?" cried Rebecca's mum as she ran towards them.

"They'll be fine now, the birds won't attack again!" said Mason with authority.

Rebecca tried to hold back her tears. The speed with which the birds had attacked had scared her. She rubbed her eyes and sniffed. Danny too, looked shaken; the colour had completely drained from his cheeks and he was trembling slightly.

"Phew! That was close!" he said.

"It was more than close! It was scary… they were evil!" said Rebecca, shuddering.

Her mum put her arm round her and gave her a cuddle. She tried to do the same to Danny, but being shy; he smiled and moved slightly ahead of them.

"I've never seen anything like that before," Mum said, "What on earth made them do it, Mr Mason?"

"Oh! They were probably spooked by something – maybe they were protecting a nest."

"Well! They certainly spooked us!" said Danny.

They walked quietly home. Mum had bought them an ice cream each to make up for the terrible incident. They didn't really enjoy them, the birds had subdued their mood and they wondered what would have happened if Mason had not been there. Mum was still trying to cheer them up by chatting all the way home, but it just made them feel worse.

Next morning Rebecca reflected that she had slept well; that at least was a relief. She was still thinking about the clue as they drove into the car park opposite the church. Rebecca sighed. Mum wanted her to go with them to church this week, but she felt sad coming to this church. It reminded her of Granddad's funeral. She shook herself and tried to block it from her mind. They walked up the steps to the doorway of St George the Martyr. The congregation was mostly old ladies like Grandma, except for one or two escorted by their husbands. There were only a couple of other children there, the organist's granddaughter and two small kids.

The service began, but her mind was fixed on the clue. Soon the boring bit came-the sermon. It was a bit complicated and she drifted into her own thoughts. As she daydreamed, she gazed around the church. She looked at two banners, one was the Mother's Union flag, with a beautiful embroidered picture of Mary and baby Jesus; the other a more exciting one, of St George fighting the dragon. Shards of coloured light played along the white of the altar cloth, looking like beautiful glimmering jewels. The beams of light drew her attention to the stained glass windows. The Last Supper, St George and the dragon were colourful, but there were also two boring looking saints, standing in benediction. The saints were standing together and at the feet of one was a *swan*... She couldn't believe it and she allowed a small cry of excitement to escape, as she jumped up and down on her pew. There, in gothic script, was written "St Oswald". Mum looked at her and raised her finger to her lips to remind her to be quiet. Rebecca settled down again, but inside her mind was in turmoil.

She took in a sharp breath as she noted the other saint's name. St Cuthbert. She knew that Cuthbert was a monk... could *he* be Oswald's friend? She couldn't wait for the service to end, so that she could get home and go online to find out about the saints.

After the service, Mum and Grandma seemed to

take ages chatting to the old ladies they knew. The rotund and jolly vicar was standing at the door to say goodbye to everyone. He always made Rebecca think of a modern day Friar Tuck. As they moved nearer, Rebecca looked at some of the old pictures on the wall near the vestibule. She couldn't believe what she saw next.

CHAPTER 10

THE VOW

As John Stell lay quietly on his palette that night his mind was busy with questions and thoughts. It still amazed him that he had been chosen to take on such a task, to be a guardian of such a treasure was a great honour. But then, was not this the sin of pride emerging again?

He had been shown the treasure and was astonished by its beauty, but it was more than that, it had power and an energy that could be felt even in the air. He needed no convincing that this object had special properties and he could only imagine what power could be unleashed in the wrong hands.

The responsibility weighed heavily on him. He knew his destiny was tied to its existence and he must protect it. The two of them were bound together for eternity. He could not see into the future but knew that to protect his burden he would need to ensure its safe keeping long into the future.

The bell rang for vigils. Brother John threw off the rough woollen blanket and rose from his cot. He slipped on his leather shoes and smoothed down his crumpled habit. He followed the other monks through the dimly lit dormitory and down the night stairs into the chancel.

He knelt on the cold stone floor and began his devotions. His mind wandered back to his task and he could hardly wait for daybreak, when he could seek out Robert the Mason.

The two men met at the packhorse bridge in Ennis Woods. Robert was a tall, powerfully built young man, whose large shovel like hands betrayed his work. He was head and shoulders taller than John, but bowed his head reverently. Although he was not a brother, he was an important member of the community. His craft was that of a mason and his work was much in evidence throughout the abbey. He belonged to the abbey as much as the stone statues he carved and even before he was appointed the protector of the treasure, he was bound to the very foundations of the great monastery.

John and Robert were drawn to each other immediately, with an affinity usually only old friends feel. They knew their duties and were aware of their gravity.

"We must seal our partnership for all time, Robert…" Stell suggested.

"Aye! That we must, but what can be sworn upon, to make our pledge true, Brother?"

"Follow me to the abbey church and I will tell thee."

The church was quiet and empty, but before too long the quire monks would be thronging for the next service of the day. They had but a short time to cement their pledge. Brother John led Robert to the Cuthbert Chapel, where an ornate sarcophagus rested. Robert recognised it as some of his own work. He instinctively reached out his hand and lovingly traced the shape of the swan he had carved only recently.

"Lay your right hand upon this sacred stone, it contains the precious treasure we are bidden to protect... swear with me to protect it at all cost, even unto death... and beyond... how say ye, Robert the Mason?" proclaimed Stell solemnly.

"Aye, master... I do swear to protect and save the treasure e'en to death and beyond..."

The two men placed hands upon the sarcophagus and silently prayed for strength... a warm energy hummed beneath their palms suffusing, their bodies. They became one with the treasure and it became one with them... their pledge was sealed and so was their future.

CHAPTER 11

FINDING

There was an assortment of old photos of serious looking Victorian gentlemen and ladies and one of St George's when the surrounding houses still looked new. The last frame held an old plan of the church and a small map of the vicinity. Rebecca's mouth dropped open, the church stood on the hill, just as it did now, but instead of being called St George's Hill, it was called... *Rabbit Hill.* She had never heard it called that before.

So, the final part of the jigsaw slotted into place. She had discovered where and who... now she needed to find why. As soon as she arrived home she went onto the computer. She looked up the saints and the swan... it took some time to find what she was looking for, but finally she did. She printed off the bits she needed and then ran over to Megan's.

Danny had seen Rebecca running across the road and into the garden and knew it must be important. He followed her to Megan's.

"Rebecca knows who Oswald is and where Rabbit Hill is!" cried Megan excitedly.

"Whoa! How did you find that out – you've been to church all morning?"

"It's *because* I've been to church that I've found out!" exclaimed Rebecca.

"Ho! Why did an angel fly down and tell you or something?" he quipped.

"Not quite, smart arse! But you're not too far off!" retorted Rebecca.

She then told them about the revelation at church and what she had discovered from the internet.

"It says that the swan is a symbol of Christian prayer and purity... but it also traces back to Pagan mythology too."

"What's Pagan?" asked Megan.

"Erm... its sort of religion and stuff before Jesus I think," suggested Rebecca.

"So, old then?"

"Erm... Oswald... he's a northern warrior King who became a saint because of his bravery in fighting the Vikings. He was beheaded and someone hid his head... wait for this... St Cuthbert had it taken to Lindisfarne and is often pictured with the King's crowned head... and because he was so good he attracted wild creatures... otters AND..."

"SWANS!"

"Yes! And wait... he's pictured as a bishop with swans... and he travelled all over the north founding churches and abbeys and his monks carried his coffin round the north for seven years to keep his body safe from the heathens."

"Phew, so... what's it all mean?"

"The treasure must be St Cuthbert's... it says the swan is his... *not* Oswald's..."

"What sort of treasure could a monk have?" asked Danny reasonably.

"I'm not really sure, 'cos they aren't allowed money or possessions."

"We get closer, but then there's a riddle and we don't have the solution."

"I think there are a few things to go on..." said Rebecca.

"What exactly?" demanded Danny.

"There's the saint thing... we need to find out if Cuthbert ever came to our abbey... or any churches near here. And we need to see if they left any relics or stuff, 'cos they kept them in abbeys, didn't they?"

"Wow! It's a bit complicated... I hope you're up to this Beccs!" sighed Danny.

That afternoon Rebecca was as good as her word, she had a long discussion with her mum about the abbey and St Cuthbert. By three o'clock Rebecca had so much information she didn't know what she was going to do with it all.

The children met later to discuss her findings and slowly, the information began to make more sense. St Cuthbert had travelled around the north of England, taking the word of God to all who would listen. He founded churches and many villages claimed that he had been responsible for their churches, including St Cuthbert's at Aldingham. There was one theory that his bones were rescued by the monks after his death and carried into Cumbria to save them from the Vikings.

"It says here, that he also saved many holy relics

from marauders," said Rebecca, "Maybe that's what the treasure is?"

"Well, we've got to go then haven't we?" said Danny excitedly.

"Where?" asked Megan.

"ALDINGHAM!"

Chapter 12

The Sacred Place

A few days later George visited his Grandparents at Ravenglass. Granny was a plump, little woman with a twinkle in her old blue eyes. Granddad was another kettle of fish, gruff and taciturn, but with a soft spot for George. George often wondered how they had lived together for so long, as they seemed to have little in common, apart from their twelve children and ever growing family of grandchildren.

George had been charged with taking Granddad's "bait" up to Muncaster Castle where he was working on the drawing room ceiling. Auntie Ginny had put up two lunches, so that they could eat together. He ran under the railway bridge towards the main road and down the path to the castle. He glanced through the window and saw Granddad working from the scaffolding. Granddad slowly climbed down the ladder and came outside to meet his grandson. The two sat on the low wall overlooking the Esk.

"Eh lad, th'as brought me bait, hast tha?"

George nodded, "Aye, Auntie Ginny said I can stop with you and have some too."

"Ah, so that's it, what's she give' us then?"

There were two huge teacakes, thickly buttered, a

hank of cheese and an apple a piece. This was washed down with tea from the Billy can. When they had finished, Granddad took out his pipe and slowly began filling it with strong fragrant tobacco. He lit it and began sucking the end to draw the tobacco. He sat smoking quietly, the coils of smoke wafted past George and he basked in the aromatic smell, which he would forever associate with his grandfather. The old man looked at George and smiled beneath the heavy walrus moustache he sported. Soon enough George pulled out the little carving from his pocket, asking what Granddad thought of it. The old man held it, stroking its contours and inspecting it from every angle.

"It's old, lad. Where didst tha find it?"

"On Piel Island, near the ruins."

He considered it for a moment. "It's not from there, it's the wrong stone. This is limestone, not red sandstone… it's come from further along the coast I reckon."

"Do you think it's a parson or a bishop?" asked George.

"Nay, lad. I think it's a more important fella than that… mebbe a saint," he answered, shaking his head.

"A saint! Can you tell which one?"

"Nay… least, not unless tha knows what church or chapel it's from. It's mebbe come outa one o'parish churches."

"Crumbs! I wonder which one, Granddad?"

"I reckon somewhere like Ulverst'n, *Gert Ossick** or even Aldin'ham… none of 'em are sandstone… and as fer saints, well, I heard tell that St Cuthbert come up

*Great Urswick

here and founded a lot of churches. He come up t' Kirkby and St Bees and set up churches there... anyway, tha needs t' keep it safe, it's a precious l'ile statue."

On the train home, George thought about what he had been told and determined that a visit to the library was definitely needed.

The next day he hunted through books about churches and the abbey, until he found what he had been looking for. He jumped up in triumph and slammed the heavy book shut, with a bang, attracting a stern look from the librarian. Aldingham did indeed date back to early Christian times and was named for St Cuthbert. The information on the saint told of him being accompanied by otters and swans. Importantly, the church was right by the sea overlooking the sands of Morecambe Bay. Everything was beginning to fit together like a jigsaw puzzle, even if a few pieces were still missing.

He and Sid set out for Aldingham. George was so excited he streaked ahead on his bike, leaving Sid far behind him. They walked up the short path to the church door and into the porch. Carefully, they lifted the latch and pushed open the heavy wooden door. The boys took off their caps as they had been taught; pushing them into their shorts pockets and they slowly walked into the cool, quiet church.

"What we looking for George?" whispered Sid.

"I dunno exactly... look for summat to do with the little statue I suppose."

Sid frowned. They split up and walked around the church, looking at the inscriptions on the walls and the windows and inside the pews. After half an hour they gave up and sat in a pew at the back of the church.

They continued to look around, hoping that something would jump out at them. They stood up and prepared to leave. As they shuffled towards the door, a beam of refracted light fell across the stone floor, from the stained glass window next to the font. They followed its source and looked up at the window… the figure on the window echoed the little figure and underneath was the inscription, "St Cuthbert."

"This has got to be good; it's him, the little fella!"

"Yes but it doesn't really get us anywhere, does it?" offered Sid.

George was already looking at the window, in the hope that it held a clue. He stood on the plinth of the scallop decorated font to see if he could get closer. He suddenly slipped and fell, banging his back against the base.

"Ow! That hurt!" he yelped.

As he rubbed his back he suddenly caught sight of something interesting. At the base of the opposite wall there were carvings. He felt the shape of the stone and traced the contours with his finger tips. A piece of the carving was missing, leaving a rough edge. George pulled the figure out of his pocket and tried to match it to the rough edge. He moved it around and then shouted in triumph. The piece fitted perfectly.

"Well, what does that prove?" Sid asked, disappointed.

Before George could answer, Sid cried out again.

"Look! It's the same little man, just over there, on

the wall... and there's a swan again!"

George looked where Sid was pointing. Adjacent to the font was a range of relief carvings. Sure enough, the same image appeared and was attended by a swan, flexing its wings. The carving looked as clean and fresh as the day it was carved, amazing in its detail. George reached out to touch the carving and followed its contours with his fingers. He pressed and pushed and the stone felt hard and cold beneath his touch. He ran his hands down to the swan's long neck, as his fingers travelled along the wings and up to the chest of the swan, he noticed a carved collar at the base of the neck. There was a cross carved on it and as he placed the flat of his hand on it, the relief image gave way beneath the pressure.

As the swan sank, a low rumbling noise came from beneath it. The stone slid back, leaving a gap, just big enough to slip a hand in. George did just that and pulled out a small package, bound in a leather bag. As he let go of the swan, the stone slid back into place, showing no clue of it ever having moved.

The boys were about to investigate the discovery further, when they heard the latch of the big wooden door slowly lift. They jumped to their feet and George pushed the package down the front of his shirt. A tall, thin pinched man entered. Something about his presence made the boys shiver. He looked directly at them, with unblinking, reptilian eyes. It was the man they had seen at Piel. They moved away from the panel, instinctively.

"What do we have here, young gentlemen?" he said in a silky voice.

"Nowt, mister… we're just looking round the church!" said Sid defensively.

"And *what* are we looking for, exactly?" he persisted.

"We aren't looking for anything… we're just looking round," said George.

"Unusual interest for such young people, are you sure you aren't trying to find something?"

His piercing eyes sliced open their minds, almost revealing their thoughts. They stood closer together, feeling safer that way. The man looked them up and down slowly and his eyes seemed to rest on George's shirt front. George automatically pulled his cap from his pocket and held it in front of him, protectively. The man registered the movement and looked hard into the boy's eyes.

"I do hope you haven't taken anything from this wonderful, old church…"

Before George could answer, the door opened again and two middle aged ladies entered, carrying armfuls of flowers. They smiled and greeted the man, glancing at the two lads. They explained that they would be decorating the church and engaged the man in a conversation that he didn't really wish to take part in.

The two boys quietly slipped out into the sunlight, butterflies of anticipation welling up inside them as they ran for their bikes. They looked behind them and pushed off up the lane, heading for Scales village. They sped off up the hill as fast as they could go, trying to put distance between them and the strange man.

The man took some time to free himself from the two very polite but chatty ladies of the flower committee. Finally, he walked briskly out of the church and into the narrow lane next to the churchyard. He looked up and down the lane in both directions, but could see no trace of the boys. Muttering beneath his breath, he ran to his smart black Morris motor car. He cranked up the engine and then set off at speed onto the new road. He was very annoyed that the boys had vanished...very annoyed indeed. He knew that they had found something... something that he wanted and must acquire at any cost.

CHAPTER 13

THE PASSING

The plain song from the chapel filtered through the rood screen to the simple infirmary ward like sunlight through the trees. Brother John was warmed by the rich smooth voices and his spirit lifted momentarily. Robert Mason huddled on a wooden stool close to the palette bed which had become John's refuge these last days. He had been fixed to the stool for many a long hour, not wishing to leave his master... and friend. John turned to Robert and smiled. Many years had passed since their pledge to each other and to the abbey treasure. Both men were aged now, but John was fading very fast, he had had the fever in the winter months and Robert had hoped his friend would improve with the warm spring. A terrible cough had wracked his thin frame ever since and it soon became clear that John was unlikely to recover.

Brother John slipped into a fitful sleep. He was troubled deeply, knowing that soon the time would come to entrust his task to another. Robert's son had been apprenticed as a stone mason and as such became tied to the abbey as his father had been. He knew of the heavy responsibility awaiting him and was prepared to carry out the duties to the best of his ability. John had watched the boy grow and believed that he could be trusted, but he had become aware of a malevolence surrounding the abbey. His uneasy mind created nightmares which showed the treasure attacked by a cloud of black birds, wings flapping furiously until the sarcophagus disappeared under a dark shroud of feathers. He awoke with a jolt.

The sudden movement roused Robert, who reached out anxiously to the old monk.

"What ails thee Brother?"

John took in a deep breath and shuddered. He turned to look at the mason.

"We need to be sure of the treasure. It must be safe! Thy son must beware of those who would steal the treasure!"

Robert shook his grey head, "Nay Brother, none will dare touch the sacred prize and the lad is wary... he'll not let thee down!"

"He must be certain to pass the knowledge on with care... there must be no mistake. I must remain to help... we must prepare to guide them into the future!" his voice rose in panic.

"Rest thyself Brother John, we have made provision... the preparations are in hand. When thy time comes ye will lie in the hallowed ground behind the high altar."

"And the sign? This is in hand?"

"Aye, as ye instructed, a stone sealed with a sacred swan... now rest..."

The monk relaxed momentarily and a deep sigh took away his anxiety. His face glowed and became young again. A mysterious energy filled him and he raised himself from the bed. He pointed at the wall; Robert looked but could not see what Brother John had seen. The monk slumped and fell back onto the bed, the colour draining from his face. A luminescence fluttered like a perfect white butterfly above the monk's inert body and then disappeared. He was at peace and Robert knew that his weary soul had gone.

Robert the Mason gazed at his old friend's face and a single tear rolled down his cheek. He brushed it away and as he did so a warm, bright light illuminated the dark infirmary.

When he turned, an amazing vision filled his heart and mind. A wonderful golden light shimmered and radiated and in the centre was his friend. The monk turned, smiled and diminished. The light exploded in luminosity and within its heart could be seen a swan.

CHAPTER 14

HIDE AND SEEK

It was fun cycling down the wide coast road and they stopped to buy ice creams. Danny, Rebecca and Megan reached the church at midday and propped up their bikes against the church wall. They noticed a boy sitting on the wall, swinging his legs. He smiled at them and waved.

They sat down on the beach in front of the church and spread out their lunches. The boy was still watching them and he made them feel uncomfortable. Rebecca whispered, "I feel a bit tight, should we ask him to join us?"

She looked over at him again and he smiled, still swinging his legs.

"We won't be able to talk though will we? We don't know him… we can't tell him why we're here," hissed Danny.

The boy was still looking. Rebecca called to him to join them.

He grinned and jumped down onto the cobbles with a clatter. The children all looked at his shoes. They had never seen anything like them. He noticed they were looking and he shrugged.

"D'ya like me clogs then? I'm the only one in me class that wears em."

They all agreed that the clogs were different and unusual. He seemed pleased with their response and sat down beside them.

They discovered the boy came from Barrow, like them. His name was George and he went to a school in town and was eleven. The children couldn't help but notice that his clothes were a little scruffy and well worn. He seemed a happy boy and told them about his family and his jobs that he did to help out. Rebecca couldn't help thinking how lucky they all were. She knew that she was well provided for, but had never really thought that anyone would have to work to help out their parents.

When they had finished their lunches, they packed away the remains into their backpacks. They told George that they were going into the church to look around.

"What' you looking for?" he asked.

They froze, for a second.

"Nothing in particular, just looking round..." said Rebecca.

"You're not looking for a swan then?" he grinned.

They halted, shocked.

"Don't worry... *I know*! I've been waiting for you... for ages..."

None of them moved a muscle. They looked at him, as if for the first time. His clothes were not just scruffy, they were old... old fashioned! Suddenly, everything became as clear as a mountain stream... this boy... was *the* boy, that Mason had told them about – the one who began the quest a long time ago.

"How did you know?"

"Just knew! Like I said I've been waiting, Mason said you'd help."

The children gaped at him. If he knew Mason... how old was Mason? None of it made sense... it was as though they were out of time... or time was muddled! He told them about the sinister thin man and his and Sid's escape.

"Hey! It sounds like Mr Steele, from the abbey," said Danny.

"Yeah, but how can it be... he couldn't be here now, not if he was here a long time ago..." said Danny.

"Well George is... when did the quest start, George?" asked Rebecca.

"1934 – that's my time."

"I don't get it... are you a ghost then?"

"Nah... pinch me... I'm real enough... but I'm not here all the time. Something happened to stop me finishing the quest, but I don't know what I did... after I put the message in the stone at Red River Road. I hid the book, but I don't know where."

"So how are you here now?"

"Dunno. It just happened. I was tired and the only thing I could think of was the quest and that I'd left it unfinished. I hadn't thought of it for so long... then, I suddenly found myself here! I don't know exactly what's happened but it's like I've got another chance."

Danny, Megan and Rebecca went into the church to look around, George lingered at the gate.

"Well, I'll see ya later. I've got to get back..."

The three turned to wave, but he disappeared as mysteriously as he had appeared.

At the end of the holidays, a few weeks later, Mum took Megan and Rebecca to a special event in the abbey grounds. A wave of hope had swept through the country that summer. Everywhere you looked there was stuff about "Making Poverty History". People were doing things to publicise this idea and most kids sported the smart plastic wrist bands, to tell everyone that they supported the idea.

The two girls chattered with excitement as they walked down the green slope towards the nave. People were already congregating there and there was a buzz of optimism as people talked to folk they didn't know and welcomed those they did. Many people were there out of curiosity. Rebecca's mum saw someone she knew and sat with them on a picnic blanket. The girls walked across the paving; weaving through the clusters of adults and children, they caught sight of Danny and his brother, Luke. They were there with the Scouts. Danny waved and walked towards them. The girls pushed their way through a carnival drum band, dressed in exciting and colourful costumes and playing extremely loudly.

The singing started and then everyone joined in. They suddenly noticed someone else – Mr Mason on the other side of the church, resplendent in his green overalls and white safety helmet. He was singing heartily from his hymn sheet, his deep booming voice resounding across the nave of the church. He was oblivious and did not see them trying to attract his attention. They moved through the crowds, pushing and jostling, losing sight of him.

Across the nave, sitting on top of a broken column, was George. He had already seen them and was beckoning them to come over. They worked their way through the crowd, but it was very difficult, as everyone seemed intent on getting in their way. They moved to the back of the crowd and began walking towards George's pillar. As they reached the grass, a sinister shadow fell across their path.

A sudden chill ran down their spines. Horrified, they looked at the originator of the shadow, Mr Steele. He blocked their path and stared coldly at them. Megan jumped involuntarily. He seemed pleased at their reaction, smiling maliciously.

"We meet again. I do hope you are behaving yourselves today."

"Course we are… we're just going to see a mate of ours…" interjected Danny.

"I don't think you should be mixing with that young man… he is a trouble maker and you will only get into trouble yourselves."

"I don't know what you mean. We're not going to do anything that will get us into trouble," argued Danny.

This annoyed Mr Steele intensely. His face hardened and he narrowed his eyes,

"You don't know what you are getting into, young man! You're dabbling with things you don't understand. If you have taken anything from this abbey, you must give it back, it belongs to me…"

As he spoke he reached out for Danny's arm. The children pulled away from him and ran around the other way. The girls tripped over each other and bumped into a lady holding a toddler. They apologised and slipped behind her. They were trying to see where George was, because he had disappeared from the top of the pillar. They ducked in and out of the people, keeping a weather eye on Mr Steele, who followed them at a discreet distance. They ran into the cloister and through the passage way to the stream.

As they ran they could hear the congregation singing in the distance and went through the gateway to the back of the abbey. They turned towards the museum and banged straight into another figure, and they saw with relief that it was Mason.

"We can't find George… and Mr Steele was there…" gasped Rebecca.

"Don't worry, you are safe and so is George. But move quickly… follow me and do exactly as I say."

It was wonderful to be taken charge of. They felt secure and knew they could trust Mason to keep them safe from Mr Steele.

Mason marched on towards the abbot's house. They had to run to keep up with him. They came to a halt at the outer wall and walked down the slope to the drainage tunnel. There, crouched under the arch was George. He grinned at them and beckoned.

"Come on, you'll be safe in here."

Mason gestured for them to go into the tunnel and told them to follow George.

Danny scrambled down into the tunnel, the others

followed. They edged along the wall apprehensively, it looked old and they weren't sure how safe it was.

"Come on!" said George impatiently, and he started scrambling along the tunnel. Although it was wide, it was not tall and they were forced to walk with their knees bent and their heads down.

"I don't get this!" said Megan, "What's the point of us going through this tunnel? If we come out the other end, we'll nearly be back to where we started."

"You'll see! Just carry on and don't talk so much!" said George.

"Cheek!" said Megan indignantly.

The children emerged at the other end in a few minutes. They crept out and stretched as they stood up. George stood with his arms crossed in front of his chest, smiling widely. The others looked at him, puzzled. They looked around. All was quiet. The abbey looked the same… but different… it was hard to put your finger on what was different. It was much, much quieter than when they had gone through the tunnel.

"Oh my God!" exclaimed Rebecca, "It's… its odd! Look! The trees are smaller… the walls look, well… cleaner, or something!"

"And where is everyone?" croaked Megan nervously.

The abbey did indeed appear different. There were iron railings and fencing where there had been none. Vegetation grew in a natural, untidy way on the masonry. The trees and grass were different too. Some trees were smaller, whereas some were growing where there had only been stumps and mounds before. George giggled at their puzzled expressions.

"You really don't get it, do you?" he asked, "You can't guess what's happened can you?"

"Er… no!" said Rebecca, shaking her head.

"What *do* you mean?" asked Danny in an exasperated voice.

"Well! Look!" He said pointing around him. "You're here! You're in *my* abbey!"

"*Your* abbey?" asked Rebecca.

"Yes! *My* abbey, *my* time!" he was jumping up and down, "You're safe here – they won't know you're here yet… and when they do you can go back through the tunnel to YOUR time!"

The others stared at him as though he was mad. Slowly the realisation dawned and shock showed on everyone's faces.

"WELL! Do you get it now?" George was losing patience.

"So you're telling us… we are in 1934?"

"Yes! At last!"

Rebecca's face paled and Megan's bottom lip trembled. Danny shook his head in disbelief and grimaced as he took in what George had said.

"What d'y mean? How can we be in 1934?" he snapped, worry rippling across his face.

"Oh no! What if we can't get back… we'll never see our mums and dads again…" Megan began to cry. Rebecca's eyes filled with tears too and Danny had paled.

George looked crestfallen.

"Aw! I thought you'd like to see where I'm from… I never thought you'd be *scared*!"

"Well, it is scary, George. Things just *don't* happen like this." Rebecca put her arm around Megan to comfort her.

"But Mr Mason wouldn't have sent you here if it wasn't safe would he?" he said, trying to comfort them.

They walked slowly and apprehensively around the grounds, towards the cloister, they were still in shock, but at least Megan had dried her tears. They continued until they reached the nave, where minutes before there had been a congregation of people. It was now empty, apart from two ladies at the far end of the church, looking at a guide book. They wore calf length, straight dresses, and both sported jaunty hats and gloves.

"Phaw! They look a bit posh!" said Megan, her curiosity distracting her.

"Why? What d'y mean?" asked George.

"Well, they look a bit smart to be going round the abbey and they're wearing hats and gloves, like they're going to a wedding or something!"

"Ladies **wear** hats and gloves, my Mam **never** goes out without a hat!" explained George.

Megan shrugged.

"Anyway, you're safe here at the moment… even if it's strange!"

They nodded and followed George to the nave. A curl of smoke rose from the chimney of the custodian's cottage, just as it had on the day they met Mr Mason. The door was ajar and there was a gate in place of the railings. What was more; a familiar figure perched, hawk-like on a stool outside the hut, smoking a pipe. He cut a dashing figure in a smart, navy blue uniform and peaked cap, looking rather like a policeman. He looked up and acknowledged them, with a wave of his pipe.

Relief replaced their anxiety. Soon they told him of the danger they had been in earlier... and of the strange turn of events which brought them there.

"Take your time, everyone..." he said comfortingly.

They all shouted at once, Mr Mason couldn't tell what they were all saying and he held up his hand to quieten them.

"We've been trying to solve the quest... but Mr Steele tried to stop us getting to George and then he brought us here... to the olden days! And it's scary!" said Rebecca in a rush. "We will get back home, won't we?" she added anxiously.

"But *you* should know... *you* sent us down the tunnel... didn't you?"

Mason nodded slowly, drawing on his pipe, smoke slowly curling around his head.

"Yeah! And we don't even know what the flipping treasure is anyway... so how can we find something we don't even know?" added Danny, exasperated.

George pushed his hands into his pockets and sighed, looking down at the floor.

"And I s'pose it's my fault. After all, I'm the one who lost the book. What are we going to do?"

Mr Mason took his pipe out of his mouth and pointed it at George, "It was no fault of yours lad. You need to think hard about where you might have hidden the book. Trace your steps back to when you left the message in the stone."

The children all sat quietly thinking, trying to imagine the route George must have taken. Danny jumped up suddenly.

"Why don't we take a walk now and see if we can jog his memory?"

"That seems a sensible idea," Mason agreed, "But you need to beware, they will be looking for you here, too. If they see you, go back to your own place and time as soon as you can."

CHAPTER 15

THROUGH THE TUNNEL

The children walked towards the gate, trembling with excitement and fear in equal measure. They couldn't help laughing nervously. It felt strange that in this time they were walking through a gate which no longer existed in their own. They continued towards the amphitheatre. It was fascinating that so much was still recognisable, yet different, all at the same time. As they reached the field, they noticed that the ugly concrete toilet block was no longer there, nor was the car park.

The custodian's cottage had changed too, looking rustic and welcoming, with its thin corkscrew of smoke. The road was narrower and dusty, but the verges more abundant and green. It was startling that there was no litter, unlike their own time, when you could hardly fail to notice discarded takeaway boxes, empty cans and other items thrown from passing cars or dropped by walkers!

They slipped down the dirt path towards the railway line and crossing point, passing close to the cottage. Astonished, they gaped at the view. A working water wheel creaked and turned noisily. This didn't exist in their century.

"Cool! Just goes to show, things don't always change for the better!" said Danny.

They reached the railway crossing. The heavy, white gate looked the same. They walked briskly across the line, instinctively looking to their left and into the seventy yard tunnel. They passed the house next to the line; it was less decorative and more practical, somehow. There were chickens and other animals, plainly heard as the little group went past.

They pushed through the metal kissing gate, no longer rusty and broken, into the field.

"Do you know what's weird?" asked Rebecca.

"What?" said Megan.

"There's no noise! It's quiet except for the birds and the animals."

"So what?" added Danny.

"Well, even when it's quiet in our time… it isn't! You can hear the cars – the traffic from Abbey Road! We haven't heard a car since we've been here."

The children looked on this as a revelation and listened attentively for a minute.

"Yeah! You're right! How strange!"

George laughed, "But not many folk have cars here! Most people walk, or get the tram or the bus. I use me bike and if we go anywhere away we go on the train."

On cue, a high pitched whistle split the silence, like a loud kettle. Above them, on top of the railway embankment, a huge monster of a machine emerged from the tunnel they had recently passed.

The children jumped up and excitedly waved at the splendid, spitting steam train, as it rumbled rowdily along the rails. It was bursting with people, many of whom waved back. The faint oily smell mingled with the damp steam and hung in the air as the train passed by. The smoke shot out ash and the children rubbed their eyes as sparks flew like fireflies. Their hearts sang with joy at the wonderful sight. As it disappeared, thundering into the distance through the trees, they felt almost disappointed.

"WOW! That was AM-AZ-ING!!!" yelled Danny, emphasising each syllable.

"You don't see those every day do you?" added Megan.

"I do!" laughed George.

"You are SO lucky! I've seen one at Haverthwaite, but to see one working on this line! WOW!" Danny added.

They began to realise how different their two worlds were. Down the valley, there were more trees scattered about than they were used to. The trees that they did recognise seemed different. Danny hit on what it was. Some were very old and must have been felled by 2005, but those they recognised were smaller and younger.

"It's like a wood!" said Danny.

"That's why I like it here. You can see the birds and I like to climb the trees and hide," said George thoughtfully.

The children all looked at each other and then again at George. He looked bemused.

"What?" he asked.

"What's your favourite tree, George?" asked Rebecca urgently.

"It's the old oak, up by the bridge, where the trains go over the river," he replied.

"Come on then! What are we waiting for?" said Rebecca.

George sprang into action, running towards his favourite tree. It stood on the bank above the river, old and gnarled, with a huge trunk and twisted roots running deep into the ground, anchoring it soundly.

George rushed over to investigate, touching the rough bark and examining the roots. He looked at it this way and that, trying to find an answer.

"Could you have hidden the book here?" asked Danny.

"I don't know. I told you I can't remember. I might have done!" He shrugged and looked up at the old tree. In a second he shinned up the trunk like a monkey, to the lower branches. He looked down at them and grinned.

"Come on then! Or are you lot too soft to climb trees?"

They needed no further invitations. They began to climb up into the tree's canopy.

"I still don't remember. But I play here a lot. Me and me mate, Sid. It's a brilliant tree. It has knots and holes and I think its holl…"

"HOLLOW?" interrupted Danny.

"Quick! Show us where the holes are…"

George pulled himself up to a higher branch and lay down its full length. He reached down towards the trunk and slipped his hand down to indicate a gap where the branch met the trunk.

"I can't feel a thing, but it feels hollow. I'm sure if I did chuck it in here we won't get it back."

They all looked crestfallen for a moment.

Suddenly, Rebecca cried, "We might not get it back *now* but what about later! Much later… in our world? Now?"

George said, "Well, it's a start…"

"What do we do now? I'd like to look up the lane to see where our houses are… or rather, *will* be," asked Danny.

"I don't know. Do you think it's safe to leave the abbey?" said Rebecca.

"Yeah ! Why not?"

However, before they could investigate, something distracted them. In the distance they noticed a figure. Across the middle of the field, buried beneath the grass, was the remnant of an abbey wall and a monk stood beside it. They paused momentarily. Even after the strange day they had experienced, it still unnerved them to see a fifteenth century monk in full daylight. George however, paled.

"Oh no, not *him* again… I saw him when I was delivering to the big house."

"Don't worry, George. He's safe! He protected us from some really creepy creatures…"

"Creatures?"

"Yes! They came looking for us…" said Danny.

"What creatures?"

"Like monkeys or something… horrible things!" shuddered Rebecca.

"So they *were* real! I've seen them!" George shivered

too, at the memory. "Why's he here? *They're* not around now are they?" He looked around quickly.

The children walked towards the monk. He turned and walked towards the abbey. The followed him quietly at a distance. They lost sight of him in the trees by the railway line. As they neared the line, a dark cloud scudded across the sky. They felt a sudden chill, on an otherwise sunny day. A slight wind stirred the leaves, the rustling echoing ominously.

Nobody dared speak. The only sound was the wind. Then, slowly, there came a fluttering from the branches. They hurried their pace, branches cracking beneath their feet, announcing their presence to whoever was listening. As they reached the roadside a single magpie swooped just above their heads, almost touching them. Megan and Rebecca squealed in fear. Danny and George swiftly grabbed their hands and pulled them along.

The magpie followed them. Two more swooped and flapped closely. They were almost at the gate, when Rebecca fell. She cried out in pain and the others rushed to help her. The magpies took advantage and attacked the group. Their hearts sank. A grey faded figure appeared.

The monk raised a hand, as he had before that night in the close. The children scrambled to their feet. He smiled kindly and ushered them past. The magpies cackled, flapped fiercely into the air, turned and flew into the trees on the other side of the road. They roosted, malevolently watching the children. The monk stood between them and the magpies, silently protecting them. They ran as hard as they could until they reached the abbot's house. They skidded and slid down the slope and into the drainage tunnel. No one stopped until they reached the other end. At the entrance, panting and catching their breath, they hardly dared emerge into the daylight.

After a few moments, George spoke.

"I'm going to stay here for a bit, until it quietens down. Then I'll go back to my place."

"What if the birds are still there?" asked Rebecca.

"Oh, I'll wait a bit. They'll be gone when I leave… don't worry."

They said goodbye and crept out of the tunnel. They wondered when they would see George again. As they walked towards the nave of the church, they noticed people moving towards the museum exit.

"It's over… how long have we been away?" whispered Megan.

"Well, we seem to have been all afternoon in the other place, but it can't be *that* long, even church doesn't go on that long!" replied Rebecca.

What an adventure, and nobody had even noticed they had gone.

Voices called to them from the brow of the hill. It was their mothers. Unaware the children had been missing, the families walked home together. The children held their secret adventure close. Each of them wondered what the next few days would hold and they glanced at each other conspiratorially as they passed the bridge. The tree was there, but not as lush and lively as it had been in George's time. It looked older, less leafy and had fewer branches. It needed to be investigated, but that would have to wait until another time.

CHAPTER 16

DEEP ROOTS

They knew they had to explore the tree as soon as possible. They weren't sure whether they should do it without George, somehow it didn't seem fair.

"But we never know when he's going to appear, do we?" complained Megan.

"No. But he seems to turn up when we need help, doesn't he?" suggested Rebecca. "Perhaps if we really think about him and how much we need him, he'll come."

"What if we go back to the river tomorrow or the tunnel, where we left him? He might come," offered Danny.

It didn't take long to agree. They were concerned the school holidays were ending and that time was running out. They would have less time once school began in September.

Rebecca went to bed buzzing with thoughts and questions. She was unable to fall asleep straight away. The night was sultry again, distant thunder rumbled out at sea. Rebecca counted between rumbles to see how many miles away it was, as Granddad had taught her. It was moving closer. A bright flash of white light illuminated her bedroom and she held her breath in anticipation of the next roll of thunder. She didn't need to wait long. The huge crack rocked the walls and she shuddered, pulling her quilt tightly around her.

The rain beat rhythmically against the window. The angry growling of the thunder was deafening, the curtains rent by slashes of lightening. Rebecca stood no chance of sleeping while the storm continued. She tentatively drew up her blind and peeped out into the garden. A ziz-zag of lightening split the sky in two. The light momentarily illuminated the garden and to her dismay, Rebecca spotted the horrible creatures. They scuttled across the patio and sat hunched like small statues, watching. She pulled away from the window a little and watched, unseen through the driving rain.

They remained as still as the carvings at the abbey, strange and other worldly. They looked permanent and solid. Rebecca wondered what her mum would say if they were still there in the morning. They were guarding something, or waiting... waiting for her to lead them to the treasure!

She awoke with a start the next morning, her neck and arm aching where she had slumped into an uncomfortable sleep the night before. She raised her head above the parapet of the window and looked out. A relieved sigh escaped when there was no sign of the weird creatures. It was a beautiful, bright day. Everything was fresh and newly washed, just the sort of day to fill you with hope and expectation. Her fears melted with the warm sun of the new day.

Everyone met at Megan's house to begin their search for the book and for George. The brilliant, late summer sunlight made their spirits soar like seagulls into the electric blue sky and they were optimistic. They walked down the lane towards Bow Bridge, hoping that George would be around; it wouldn't be the same if he didn't turn up.

Reaching the packhorse bridge, they noticed branches snapped by the storm and debris dipping and bobbing below in the fast, full stream. They reached the small concrete footbridge and stopped dead as a huge stick flew out from the bushes on the other side, hitting the water with a splash. They looked in the direction of the missile and laughed when they saw George.

"Ha! Your faces! Did you think it was *them*?" he chuckled.

"I knew you'd come," said Rebecca triumphantly.

"Course I came, you can't finish this quest without me... and him!" George pointed to the figure of the monk, further down the field.

Butterflies of excitement fluttered inside them. It was still a strange sensation seeing someone from an earlier century. George they could cope with, but the monk *looked* as though he was from the olden days and it was hard not to feel a little peculiar.

They walked down towards him, but as they got closer he seemed to dim, eventually disappearing.

"He's a bit like a bad video recording isn't he – flickering on and off?" observed Danny.

"I expect that's because he comes from so long ago... he's even older than George!" said Danny.

"Hey! I'm the same age as you lot! It's just that I'm here... and then I'm not!" retorted George.

They halted at the bend in the river, where it disappeared under a tunnel beneath the railway line. The oak tree lay on its side, like a giant sleeping in the grass. Its roots had been wrenched from the ground by the force of the storm and its huge trunk was rent from top to bottom, where lightening had hit last night. It presented a pitiful picture, looking helpless and immobilised with its roots sticking out above the soil. Its thinly leafed branches were spread out across the grass, dangling the tips into the water.

"It looks like its washing its hair in the river," laughed Megan.

"Never mind its branches, just look at those roots!" exclaimed Danny.

George jumped onto the trunk. He walked along its length to the branches and leaned over to feel around the hole where he had pushed the book, all those years before. He struggled and pushed and finally removed his arm from the tree.

"It's not there! Surely, *they* can't have found it yet? Can they?" he said.

The others looked at him, panic gleaming in their eyes. Rebecca shook her head and walked to the foot of the tree.

"You pushed it into the tree, but we couldn't feel it yesterday, could we? We said the tree was hollow, well, what if it fell through to the bottom? Where would we be likely to find it now?" she reasoned.

The solution was there in front of them. George rushed over to the exposed roots. Indeed, the tree was hollow, along one side. He pushed his hand into the soil covered roots and rummaged about. Some roots were still fixed into the ground and there was a lot of leaf mould and debris. He picked up a stick and began poking about with it. After what seemed an age, he shouted, "There's something here, but it's attached to the root somehow."

They all began to help, pulling and tugging at the stubborn root. Finally, it came free, sending them all crashing into each other. The object flew from his hands onto the grass beside them. Eagerly, George picked it up and held it up.

"It's the book! It's the book!" he yelled. "Look, it's still wrapped in its piece of leather and it feels dry!"

"Well, don't let everyone know, George!" reminded Danny.

They sat awhile, hardly daring to believe that they had retrieved a clue. They decided that the best thing to do would be to examine it at home, rather than risk being seen. Danny pushed the book into his backpack and then suggested they ate their lunch.

"Thing is, we need to act normal, if we rush home now, those birds might notice. We mustn't act as if anything is out of the ordinary," said Danny.

"Well, what do I do?" asked George, "I don't know whether I should be seen at your house, it doesn't feel right somehow."

"Why not? We saw you at Aldingham, *that* was a different place."

"I know, but… what if I meet someone… or something?"

"We can cross that bridge when we come to it! We can go in our shed if you want," said Danny.

"Alright! But we need to keep our eyes peeled!"

The others weren't quite sure what they needed to keep their eyes peeled for, but it made them feel excited, like being on a secret mission. George nearly jumped out of his skin when a huge four wheeled drive sped up behind them. This was swiftly followed by two more cars, all of them careering along at breakneck speed.

"I've never seen so many motor cars. They're so massive an' all! You people must be well off…"

The others hadn't realised how different things would seem to him.

"I can't believe all these houses! All this were fields… and where's the railway line up to the mines? It's amazing this is!"

He was referring to the old iron ore mine workings, now unused.

They took him into the close and hurried him down the road to Danny's, because suddenly, he looked out of place – alien even. His clothes were shabby, old fashioned and his clogs, well, they were positively eccentric!

Reaching the shed they breathed a collective sigh of relief. Danny went to get Coke and snacks and the gang sat on the floor cushions in the shed.

"I can hardly believe that things will be *so* different, *so* rich in the future. You lot don't know you're born!"

"Why? We aren't rich at all!" argued Megan.

"Well, look at these houses! They all have gardens for a start!"

"So? Lots of people have gardens, George!" said Danny, a little defensively.

"Not in my street mate!" he laughed, "We 'ave a back yard and an outside privy!"

They soon got to the question of the book. They were ready to examine it in detail, hopefully without interruption.

The pages were faded and felt fragile to touch. The writing was ornate and beautiful, but extremely hard to read. Here and there were small drawings and maps, some more recognisable than others. On the first page was an inscription, which on close examination was easy to read.

"It's in funny language… it's English, but it doesn't sound right," said Rebecca.

"What does it say then?" asked Danny impatiently.

"These be the accounts of the followers of ye sacred brother of Lindisfarne, who hath sworn to protect that treasure in the care of the white monkes of the Monasterie de Fournes in any way appropriat to their monasterie. In this the year of our souverayne lord the Kyng Henricus VIII, 1537. All who have followed Brother John Stell kepe this sacred trust."

"It's all beginning to tie in to what we know… brother of Lindisfarne, that's Cuthbert, John Stell… the scribe with the swan from the museum," said Rebecca excitedly.

"Go on then, turn over… what's next?" urged Danny.

The next page showed a very primitive map, showing drawings of the abbey, Piel, Aldingham and all the familiar places.

They found a list of strange names and dates, beginning with John Stell himself. The others numbered monks, abbots and some ordinary looking names too. Alongside names like Willelmus de Dalton and Johannes Tourner was something vaguely familiar.

"Look! It says Robert the Mason of Park Grange!" Rebecca danced up and down excitedly, "Then, you've got Laurentius, Thomas Chambre, Brother Clement and look – *again* Johannes *Mason* of Crivelton, Thomas Snell, and Master Matthew *Masoun* of the Cloister School of the Abbaye de Fournes."

"Do you reckon Mr Mason is the same family as these Masons?" exclaimed George.

"Well, he did say there's always been Masons around the abbey, didn't he, Danny?" reminded Megan.

"So, his family *has* always been around to help… so why did George need to help? And why us?" said Danny.

"I think I get it… Mr Mason is in my time and in this time too. But that can't be right, can it? He can't be *that* old, can he? So how is he in two different places?" George pondered.

"Well, perhaps he's not the same person! Perhaps the one in your time is his dad or something!"

"No! I know Mr Mason. He's married, but he never had any kids so far as I know!" revealed George.

"Well, what then?"

"Does it mean that there was always a Mason, until… there wasn't… till Mr Mason had no kids to pass on the quest?"

"That's just what I mean! I think he needed someone to pass it on to and I was just handy… at least, the monk must have helped to choose me! But then I messed it up by getting sick and everything!"

"AND they had to find someone to replace you, too! It was probably going to be passed onto you and your family!"

They all agreed it sounded quite logical. However, it still did not solve the quest.

They continued to look at the book. There were a few significant details about past events. At these times the treasure was more at risk. The final page showed a detailed map of the abbey grounds. It was covered in tiny written notes, but some were too hard to read at all, and many places on the map the children had never heard of, not even George.

This was going to take some time to unravel and they did not know how much time they really had. George suggested they made a copy of the map and asked for a pencil and paper. They all laughed.

"It would take you ages to copy that," said Danny.

"I'm a good artist. I can do it."

"I daresay you could… but we have a better way. Come on, I'll show you!" said Danny.

George followed him into the house. When they came back ten minutes later, George was stunned. He held in his hand copies of every page.

"That machine is magic, pure magic! It's amazing!"

Danny had scanned it and printed it on the computer.

The children decided to hide the book and use the copies. They knew that these too must be guarded carefully.

It was nearly five o'clock and the children were

going to get ready for their tea. It was tempting to ask George to stay too, but he said himself it could be risky. Who knew what questions he would be asked by inquisitive parents? So, reluctantly, they decided to walk him back to the field. As they walked along the pavement towards the end of the street, the worst thing happened. Rebecca's mum called from the front door.

"Rebecca! Tea will be ready soon, don't go away."

She continued to stare at them as they walked along, craning her neck to get a better look at George. At one point Rebecca thought she was about to say something and stop them.

They quickened their pace. She watched them closely all the way along the street, peering at the newcomer as they went.

"I'm gonna get all kinds of questions now. She'll want to know who George is, where he lives, where we met him and all that stuff!"

"Just say she's seen me before! Make out I've been here before… I bet you'll be able to convince her."

They reached the old railway bridge and George turned and told them to go back. They tried to argue, but he said he would be fine. He ran down the lane towards the abbey. He turned and waved, disappearing from view.

CHAPTER 17

PROBLEM SOLVED

The map was hard to decipher and match places to the ones they recognised. Days melted into weeks and George had not returned, despite them trying to find him on numerous occasions. Within a short time, they were involved in the new school term and daily tasks which took up their spare time. The nights were drawing in, so their activities were curtailed in the evenings, leaving only weekends to solve the mystery. Each one studied their copy of the map, but to little avail.

The map was proving extremely difficult. The writing was tiny and hard to read and many of the places were totally unidentifiable. It was a problem. One damp, dismal Saturday they met up at Rebecca's to see if they could push things on further. They studied the book as they had done many times before, but were as frustrated as ever.

The abbey was obvious and the river, they could see the abbey precinct wall, and tried to place where the roads were. The land around the abbey was rural and there were plenty of wooded areas.

They could just make out where the main road would be. Abbey Road was the impressive Victorian main road into Barrow. It was wide, straight as any Roman road and lined with trees. It was of course, not there when the map was drawn. The only identifiable road was the winding lane from the east gate of the abbey. It threaded its way across the new road and split into two, following a route towards the coast and in the other direction towards Dalton. Dalton was an important town when the abbey was at its prime. The abbots built a small castle in front of the market square. At the Dissolution the abbot was given the living of the vicar of Dalton and the church became his responsibility.

They examined the little picture of the church and Danny followed the tiny path past it, running along the steep hill, down the valley. There were a couple of buildings marked, an inn and a large common area, called Goose Green. A tiny paddock was marked as the pinfold, the path ran past this and into a wooded area, roughly parallel to the main road in the present day. Suddenly, Rebecca called out; "Look!" she cried excitedly, "It says *Cuffbert's* way! The two "ff's" stand for "th", I'm sure. That's what they used to do in the olden days..."

"Yeah! D'you think it's a sign? It's that funny writing. What else can you see?" asked Danny.

They fell quiet, as they looked carefully, trying to tease out the details from the faded manuscript. The path ran straight along the boundary of the road and fell below where the railway embankment cut through the fields to the back of the abbey. They examined the features along the path, around the church and at the abbey. Adjacent to the church was a plan drawing of the small pele tower, known as Dalton Castle.

The tower still existed, though few people realised that you could visit it. The children looked carefully at the picture.

"I've been there, it's amazing. You can see for miles from the top and there are old helmets and stuff. The man let us try them on," said Danny.

They looked at each other; they had all noticed there were little drawings of statues on the roof. Beside one was a small inscription. It said, simply, "Oswald", the next was "Our Lady", then "George" and last of all, "Cuthbert".

"I think we know what we need to do next…" began Danny.

On Sunday, they set off on their bikes through the lanes. As they reached Bow Bridge, they began to talk about George. They continued up the lane towards Dalton. When they reached the brow of the steep hill, they noticed something else. Along the rim of the hill, where the old abbey wall ran, they caught sight of another figure. It was the monk. They were pleased to see him again, he held little fear for them now, and in fact it was a comfort knowing he was looking out for them. The children locked up their bikes and went to the front of the castle, which faced the church, across a small courtyard.

On the wooden door was pinned a notice.

To visit this monument, please contact Mrs. M. Rogers, 9 The Square, Dalton, between

10a.m. and 4.30p.m. Thursday, Friday, Saturday and on Sunday between 1p.m. and 4.30p.m.

They walked around the small square, examining each door. Eventually, Rebecca shouted the others over to the little white cottage, with number 9 on the gate. The cottage was as pretty as a picture postcard. The paintwork was pale blue and the last of the late summer roses adorned the porch and wall around the squat door. The iron gate squeaked musically as they went through and walked up the shrub lined, tiled path. Danny pointed in excitement to the little metal plaque on the wall. It held a date, 1625, but more interestingly, it sported a little engraving of that familiar icon, a swan.

The door creaked open. A small, neatly packaged lady held open the door and smiled. Her hazel eyes shone like ripe chestnuts, her smile lighting up her whole face.

"Hello dear. How can I help you?"

"Well, we'd like to see in the castle if that's alright, please?" replied Rebecca politely.

"Of course, I'll get the key… is it just the four of you?"

"Er… three actually," answered Rebecca.

"Can't you count Rebecca? It's four with me, you dope!" said a familiar voice from behind them.

The children turned round. There by the gate, was George. He stood, hands in pockets, grinning from ear to ear.

Mrs Rogers disappeared into the cottage, reappearing again with a huge bunch of keys, like a jailer. She scuttled past them and led the way back to the castle. They reached the castle and she fiddled with the keys momentarily, finally pushing a huge ornate key into the door. The key turned, unlocking the door with a click. The heavy door swung open easily and they followed her into the entrance.

"Are you sensible children?" she asked.

They nodded vigorously.

"Well, this is as far as I go, my old legs don't like all those steps. Mr Rogers isn't here at this time or he would give you a tour. Take as long as you like, but be careful, especially on the top floor. All the information you need is on the cards next to the exhibits. I'm sure you'll be fine… bring me the key when you're done. You know what to do… don't you George?"

She didn't give them time to answer, but disappeared as quickly as she had at the cottage. The children were left gaping at her little figure as it scurried back to her cottage.

"So she knows you George? How does that work?" asked Megan.

"Well, I've been here before… I tried to find out things and I got chatting to her. Gave me tea once…"

"Does she know about you?"

"S'pose so."

Danny interrupted, "I don't believe this… she's trusted us with a whole castle!"

"Well! Let's get on with it then!"

The first floor was a museum, with old fashioned

glass cases and all manner of strange items standing to attention around the edge of the room. They examined the contents of each and read each card to try and find further clues. They continued up the stairs to the top floor. Again each item was examined. Danny seized a Roundhead's helmet from the shelf and placed it on his head. Their laughter pealed around the tower, masking the distant echo of footsteps down the well of the staircase. By the time they heard, it was too late. The only way out was down the spiral stairs and that would bring them to the person coming up.

George instinctively hid any evidence of the book. They waited nervously, breathing quickly for the intruder to emerge. Megan gasped with horror when saw who it was and hid behind Danny.

Mr Steele smiled at the children, his thin lips pulled tightly across his rodent teeth. The effect was very discomforting and made them shudder. They packed tighter into their little huddle.

"So, we meet again," he sneered. "I did warn you not to meddle in my concerns."

"But we aren't doing anything… we don't know what you're talking about," said Danny, bravely.

"Oh, I think you do. You know exactly what I'm talking about. You may not know what you're looking for, but you're trying to find what belongs to me. It would be in your best interests to tell me what you know and leave the searching to me."

He stared hypnotically, invading their innermost thoughts. Rebecca moved towards the staircase, but Steele blocked the way.

"What do you know? What have you taken from me?" he demanded nastily.

"Nowt! We haven't taken 'owt from thee!" shouted George, pushing himself forward in front of the others.

"YOU! I might have known you would be involved. You crossed me before, boy, and I don't forget when I'm crossed. You will cooperate or you will be sorry!" he snarled. He reached towards Rebecca's bag, where the book was.

A scuffle broke out and Mr Steele grabbed the bag, pulling it off her shoulder. George jumped in front of him with a roar, to protect Rebecca. Mr Steele stumbled backwards in surprise as George launched himself at him. The others scrambled towards the stairs and raced down the spiral staircase as fast as they could go. They heard George yell behind them, "Go, get out! Run!"

They ran as though Lucifer himself was after them, headlong into a welcome figure.

"Oh Mr Mason, thank God it's you!" shrieked Megan.

"Steele's up there... "yelled Danny, drowning out the others.

Unexpectedly, George flew out of the castle door behind them, almost knocking them down like skittles. Following swiftly behind was Mr Steele. Mason stiffened, increasing in height. He physically blocked the path to the children.

"Mason! What do you think you are doing?" the man snarled, "You can't stop me! You can't be there to protect them all the time!"

"I think Mr Steele, you'll find I can... and I will!"

"You know the prize should be mine! Through the ages it should have been mine to take… John Stell was the guardian and it should fall to his kin to carry on!" he shrieked.

"*You* gave up that privilege! You and your miserable ancestors! You betrayed the memory of your honoured relative by your greed and avarice. That is why these children will protect the treasure in your stead. My forefather was entrusted long ago as custodian and I will continue until the treasure is safe. Your power is weak, ours is strong because it comes from what is right and just."

Mr Steele looked as though he would explode and his face was white with fury. Two vivid red spots appeared on his cheeks. His eyes hardened, glittering.

"You can't stop the inevitable! You're a fool, your fate is knitted up with mine and you cannot change it. You are trapped inside time just as much as I!"

He turned quickly and strode off down the hill, his coat flying behind him like black wings.

Mason turned, "Go to Mrs Roger's and wait!" he turned to lock the castle door with the big iron key. The children ran off towards the little cottage. She was waiting at the door and ushered them in briskly.

A short passage led to a cosy room lit by a tiny mullioned window. The room was old fashioned. Instead of a fire or central heating there was a black leaded kitchen range, a huge kettle was suspended above a crackling fire, steaming and whistling as it boiled. In the centre of the room was a table covered with a heavy cloth. It was laden with plates of delicious looking cakes and scones, a huge slab of butter and a crystal dish of homemade jam lay waiting to be spread on the freshly baked scones and teacakes. There were currant squares, sticky, black gingerbread, fruit cake, iced cakes and butterfly cakes. China teacups lay in readiness, with a jug of fresh milk and a matching teapot, with its lid beside it, waiting to be filled with boiling water. It looked like an afternoon tea Rebecca had once had in a posh hotel, inviting and delicious.

"Well, dears, sit down and tuck in, do you all want tea?" she asked, as if everything was as normal.

The children were too surprised to argue and sat around the table. Mrs Rogers handed them plates and gestured them to eat. As they took scones and cakes from the plates, she poured steaming hot cups of tea.

"I hope you like my good china cups. I always think tea tastes better from bone china."

The children were bemused. One moment they were in danger and the next they were sitting having afternoon tea with a homely old lady, who could be anybody's Granny.

The bewilderment continued until Mr Mason arrived. He stooped as he came in through the low door, overpowering the little room with his large frame.

"Sit you down then our Robert, you look as if you could do with a cup of tea, dear."

He looked kindly at his elderly sister and took the cup and saucer she offered him.

"Very welcome Peggy, thank you. *That* was a very close shave. Steele is very determined and will not rest until he gets what he wants."

"Maybe not, but you will discover it soon, I am sure."

"But we don't even know what it is that he wants!" answered Rebecca.

"Can't you tell us?" asked Danny.

"I know little more than you. I don't know what it is or where it's hidden… but I know if it falls into the wrong hands that time itself will spin out of control and *he* will use it for ill."

Danny and the others frowned, confused.

"You're closer than you think my dear," Mrs Rogers said, looking at him steadily with her clear blue eyes.

She knew too!

Mason smiled as if he had read his thoughts.

"Yes, Peggy is one of us. She is my sister; she is a guardian, too."

They continued their unexpected tea party, thoughtfully and in quiet peacefulness. When they had finished their tea they helped to clear the table. Once cleared, the table was stripped of its cloth and Mason rolled a large parchment out in front of them. He revealed an old map, very similar to the one in their little book.

They looked at the familiar symbols and drawings and recognised the writing style.

"I need to tell you what I *do* know of the treasure," began Mason. "A monk was entrusted with a great treasure by the abbot, chosen for his honesty, devotion and bravery. He was warned of the dangers surrounding this great treasure, of people tempted to steal the treasure and use it for gain, for evil. He left clues to help those who would protect it and made hiding places to keep it safe. Look at this one copied from the great Coucher Book," he leafed through the book until he found Latin verses which the children had not understood.

" Stella parens Solis John Stell rege munere Prolis"

It means, *O star, mother of the sun, direct the favour of your son to John Stell."*

"What *does* that mean?" asked Danny.

"It is drawing your attention to his name Stell; Stella is a play on words and means star. The rest is just asking for divine protection!"

He was entrusted with a companion, to watch the treasure and pass on his knowledge to future generations, to carry on this task. After John Stell died other monks were assigned to protect the treasure within the abbey walls. This worked well for many years, and the treasure was safe. Then the abbey itself was under threat, from the king. The last abbot hid the treasure in a place of special devising and left clues to guide those in the future. He became the vicar of Dalton and he was under great pressure to reveal its whereabouts."

"The monk in the museum… is our monk… the one we saw today? John Stell?"

"Yes!"

"Well, who was the companion then?"

"Robert the Mason he was named," answered Mr Mason.

"Robert the Mason… Robert… Mason… that's the same name as…"

"He was my ancestor. He worked in the abbey, as a mason, and each generation passed on the task. Until mine, I'm afraid…" he tailed off sadly.

His sister patted him on the knee, shaking her head. He put his hand on hers and patted it in acknowledgement.

"My sister and I each waited for the blessing of children. It was not to be and unfortunately our line was doomed to end. Of course this was important; because the task has always been passed to the eldest of our family, so we faced a dilemma… we had to find someone to take on the responsibility. Our time was limited, but we had new hope when we found George… a boy of good and honest character, but then illness stopped his quest and we were trapped. Trapped in time, until he could complete the task or pass it on."

"What do you mean? Trapped in time?" asked Danny.

"We are held here, between two worlds until the treasure is safe and its guardianship is assured. It is an object of great power. Those who possess it can move through time and in the wrong hands great evil can be wrought. Its discovery is imperative and because there is no guardian there is a rift in time itself… trapping us and allowing *them* to manipulate it and carry on different existences."

"So, you're like George… you're from the past!"

"Yes. Our time is over, but we cannot leave or pass on until our job is finished."

It became even more important to succeed now that they knew that Mr Mason's future was also at stake.

"Isn't it awful, being stuck?" asked Rebecca.

"No, dear," reassured Mrs Rogers, "We just carry on our normal lives, but sometimes we are here and sometimes we are in our own place."

"Where does Mr Steele fit in?" asked Danny

"He craves the treasure and has persuaded himself that it belongs to him."

"Why? It can't be his, if it belonged to the abbey."

"He believes because his ancestor too, was entrusted to this task that he has more right to it than anyone else."

"Who's his ancestor then?" asked Megan perplexed.

"I know… it's easy… think of his name… Steele…" Danny looked on eagerly, waiting for them to catch up.

"Steele… oh not… it can't be… Stell? Can it?" said Rebecca in disbelief.

"John Stell's family always had close connections with the abbey. By Henry VIII's time, those outside the abbey were greedy and tried to take what they could for themselves. Steele was one who has been searching for many years. Your time brings out the worst in people and honour, truth and duty mean little. Selfishness and greed has helped him to become stronger and he came close to finding the treasure in George's time."

The children were surprised at this revelation, it made him seem even more sinister, knowing that he was related, however distantly, to the honest old monk. It was a bit scary too, knowing that he was able to travel in both times as easily as George.

"So what next?" asked Danny.

"You must continue to find your way. I can only guide, as can Brother John. He has no power in this time until the treasure is rediscovered."

CHAPTER 18

TIMESLIP

Weeks passed slowly, with the same apprehension of awaiting an exam result. Danny returned to the castle often and Rebecca tried to visit Mrs Rogers, finding the cottage much changed. They assumed the cottage itself must be linked to the changes in time, just like the tunnel in the abbey – some sort of time portal.

Of George too, they had seen nothing, since he left them at the castle that day. The only indication that it had not all been a dream was the flurry of magpies which attended them whenever they moved around the countryside. Occasionally, wicked crows, rooks and ravens took the place of the magpies, silently observing their movements.

Christmas approached fast. A week before they broke up for the holidays, there was to be a Christmas festival at Dalton church. Bands and choirs joined together to celebrate and there was a special service to remember those who would not be there at Christmas. Rebecca and her family were going and she had made a tree decoration with Granddad's name on it, to hang on the tree of remembrance.

Danny and Megan were singing in the choir and Rebecca was playing the trumpet for the school band.

The night was bitterly cold, the sky cloudless and scattered with a million pinprick stars. The church windows glowed invitingly with warm, twinkling candlelight and flickering tree lights. It was enchanting and the stained glass shimmered like a myriad of jewels, filling the children's hearts with warmth.

Inside the atmosphere was friendly, people jostling each other and greeting old friends, unmet since last Christmas. The congregation settled down and the church was dimmed, illuminated only by glittering Christmas trees of all kinds and descriptions. They ranged from traditional and bizarre to positively strange. Each tree had been dressed by different groups or societies in the community, bringing their own flavour and particular brand of Christmas.

The carols began. Even the most Scrooge like audience would not be able to resist the spirit of Christmas pervading the church. At the interval, there were mince pies, mulled wine and orange. The children waved to each other and pushed their way through the long queue to the refreshments. Eventually, they met up in the vestry. When they reached the front of the queue they stopped dead in amazement when they saw who was serving at the stall.

Mrs Rogers was there, large as life, her hazel eyes shining with amusement when she saw their surprise.

"Hello, you look as though you've seen a ghost!" she joked.

"We tried to come and see you, you know?" explained Rebecca.

"Oh I know that, dear. The time wasn't right, that's all."

"Is it right now?" asked Danny.

"You bet it is, mate!" piped up a familiar voice. George sprang from nowhere.

"Now, don't waste time, now you've got it... use it well, my dear!" instructed Mrs Rogers.

Within minutes the gang moved from the vestry into the church body again. The people were oblivious as they passed and Rebecca jumped as she almost bumped into Grandma. She was about to speak, but noticed that Grandma stared right past her.

"It's like she's looking through me!"

"She is! You're not there!" explained George, pausing to put a grubby hand gently on Grandma's shoulder and squeezing it, almost affectionately. Grandma looked around quickly, as if she had heard a distant voice or seen a familiar face.

"What d'ya mean?" interrupted Danny, "Course we're 'ere."

"Yes! But they can't see us... we're between times... Mrs Rogers is here and so am I... and you're with us... we're in a fracture in time."

"I don't like the sound of that!" said Megan, her voice trembling.

"Don't worry; it will give us the time we need. They can't see us; it's safer for us – like hiding between the centuries. Steele won't know 'til it's too late."

"Cool!" said Danny, in admiration.

Megan still didn't look too sure.

The church door was open, beckoning them. As they walked past the people they could not help test to see if they really were invisible. Danny pulled grotesque faces, trying to get a response.

"This must be what being a ghost is like!" mused Rebecca.

"Yes, it's a bit odd isn't it? You must feel quite lonely not being able to speak and be heard," sighed Megan.

The children stopped in their tracks. Ahead of them the candle flickered and a small plume of grey smoke spiralled and hung, suspended in the air. The church fell silent and darkness enveloped them like a thick blanket. A heavy smell of incense filtered into their noses. The only illumination came from thick, yellow candles. The grey smoke grew denser and at its heart was a small orb of silver light. The light grew in intensity and the smoke took on a more solid form. A figure they had often seen in the distance materialised clearly before their eyes. They quaked despite themselves.

John Stell stood before them, as solid as any other person in the church. He was of medium height, and slightly built. His hair was shaved into a tonsure; face clean shaven and he smiled benignly at them. He was about fifty, but his face was weary and tired. His habit, more grey than white, was hooded, with a black scapular over the top. On his feet he wore soft leather boots. He smiled, "Welcome, my children. Ye must watch closely and ye will learn of our most precious treasure. Be sure that ye protect it well and take it where it will be safe again. Ye have done well to help thus far and ye will give Robert the Mason back his time and stop the evil ones gaining a powerful tool."

The children were too shocked to speak. He stepped back into the shadow, his outline still visible. A distant rumble came from the doorway. Commotion ensued and daylight flooded into the church. They gasped in amazement. The church was empty, not only of the people, but the trees and the furnishings were gone too. It was bare. The walls were illustrated with colourful pictures of demons and angels and scenes from the scriptures. A carved rood screen stretched across the aisle, obscuring the high altar. The church had shrunk. This was the older, medieval church and not the Victorian one they all knew. Candles in wall sconces lit the church and the windows revealed medieval stained glass. The heavy wooden doors flung open.

Men strangely dressed pushed a huge stone font balanced on what looked like a large wooden sledge, with log rollers beneath. The men struggled to move the rollers forward, edging the heavy structure nearer to them. They jumped back instinctively, but were unseen. The men wore leather jerkins and hose, with leather boots. Their hair was long to the shoulder. A man dressed in a grey tunic, shorter than the monk's, with trousers and boots below, was directing the men. They pushed and manoeuvred the heavy font into its place, beneath the big stained glass window at the back of the church.

"At least this will be safe from Holcroft and his despoilers. It will be here in this church long after old Henry is gone!" said one of the men.

The man in grey, an abbey lay brother, nodded in agreement.

"What wilt thou do Thomas Snell? Where wilt thou find work now that the abbey is gone?" asked an old man.

"I know not, some have found work as clerks and tutors and the abbot is to be vicar of Dalton. I fear there will be little left for me. My family have always put one son to the abbey and I am to be the last. Even the boys in the Cloister school will have no means to learn in the abbey. I have nothing and nowhere to go". He looked angry as he spoke and the men all shrugged in sympathy.

The scene changed seamlessly. It reminded Danny of watching news clips on television. The men were gone and the church quiet again. The light faded and dimmed, an ethereal blue light filtering through the darkened window. The door opened and an elderly man dressed in robes, stole in quietly. In his arms he carried a large package wrapped in leather. He closed the door behind him and staggered towards the font. He knelt and dropped the parcel to the stone floor. He was obscured from their view and there was a click, followed by the sound of stone grating on stone. He looked around anxiously and moved the package from sight. The sound of stones grating on stone was heard again and he stood up. He wiped his brow and walked slowly away from the font, past the children and into the body of the church, where he fell heavily to his knees in prayer.

The door opened and the man in grey came in. The

priest spun round to see who was there. Tension hung in the air like an axe waiting to fall, but the priest relaxed when he recognised the other man.

"It's you Thomas. I was concerned. I thought you may be the King's men, from Thomas Holcroft."

"Holcroft's men are lodged in the castle and are taking food and ale. They will not bother us!" he replied, walking towards Roger Pele, the abbot of Furness.

Roger Pele rose to his feet and embraced Thomas Snell warmly.

"We must repair from here to avoid their suspicions."

"Where is the treasure my Lord Abbot?"

"That, you need not know, my son. The fewer who know, the safer the treasure will be."

"I MUST KNOW!" interjected Snell. "My kinsman, the scrivener, John Stell helped to keep this treasure safe and now it can be of no further use to the abbey, so I lay claim to it."

"My son!" exclaimed the abbot in horror. "The treasure can belong to no man, not even the King. You know this. You know this is why 'tis hid' and you can gain nought from it yourself."

"You stupid, old fool! The church you served is dead and you will be too, if the King finds you have hidden a great treasure from him. Let me have it, so that I can bargain with his man Holcroft."

The abbot looked at Snell in disappointment, shaking his head.

"Ye will ne'er find the treasure and ye will ne'er

reach Holcroft to tell him of it. The people of Dalton are loyal and will prevent you, by any means they have. Ye may seek the treasure but your greed will prevent ye from finding it."

The children were hardly breathing. It was like watching a rerun of history. The scene began to fade and John Stell moved forwards. He smiled and spoke.

His tones were calm and steady, but his accent sounded strange to their ears.

"As you see, my relative hath betrayed my purpose. He and his children after him turned to avarice and no longer cherished what I once protected. Ye must find where 'tis hid and ye must find the key to open the place... safe keeping. God bless... from danger." His speech faltered and became crackly like a bad recording.

With that, the monk's image withered and vanished. At that moment the children became aware of the people milling around them again. They felt slightly dizzy and strange, but before they could collect themselves an announcement came over the microphone for performers to return to their places. They looked around for George, but he had done his usual disappearing act. They were becoming used to his comings and goings and hardly commented upon it.

Chapter 19

The Key

"We've gotta go to the church, we need to look round that font," said Rebecca.

"Well, no time like the present!" said Danny.

The sky hung heavy and overcast like a mantle, blocking the sun completely, the air brittle with the cold. They walked briskly down the lanes and tried to keep warm, their breath making little white clouds in front of them.

George was waiting by the gate at Bow Bridge. He was trussed up in a bulky looking overcoat, with a grey balaclava helmet, a scarf and knitted gloves. He still wore his customary knee length trousers, grey socks and the clogs too.

"Well, that was spooky wasn't it?" he remarked.

"You're not kidding!" said Danny, "X-Files stuff or what?"

"X-Files?" he asked, puzzled.

"It's a telly… oh, never mind!"

They trudged past the cemetery and down the steep hill into Dalton. The church tower was silhouetted above the houses, spurring them to move faster. Snow began to flutter softly, flakes floating like feathers; they jumped up, catching the flakes in their hands and on their tongues. By the time they reached the square outside the castle the snow was heavy and lay like a thick, white blanket, covering the ground and lacing the bare branches of the trees like icing.

Their track past the castle left telltale footprints in the new clean snow. The noises of the town were muffled and everything had a bright, brand new look. George tried the handle of the church door. It creaked as it moved and they pushed it open. Danny closed the door behind them, "We shouldn't take any chances!" he whispered.

They circled the font, like hungry lions around their prey, examining it for buttons and levers, but there were no clues. George touched the carvings, the abbey crest and especially the swans, but there was no indication of an opening in the stone. Megan stamped her feet to keep warm, the church was cold and still.

"Well, we aren't finding much here, are we? Let's go!" she moaned. "And I'm scared... let's go!"

"Don't be daft!" snapped Danny, "We can't give up, can we? You're always bloody scared, you're a real baby!"

"Don't call me daft! I'm not a baby either; I'm fed up with all this! I'm going home!" she flounced off, banging the door behind her.

They stared at the door in disbelief.

"Now look what you've done!" exclaimed Rebecca. She followed Megan outside.

As she turned into the path there was no sign of her. Rebecca was concerned, where had her friend gone so quickly?

Megan walked briskly up the path into the square, muttering under her breath. They were never going to solve this stupid quest. It was too scary anyway, what with monks and magpies and goodness knows what! She scuffed the new laid snow with her boots. Her gaze fell on a set of larger prints. Looking around sharply, she could see the prints had followed theirs to the church. Fear scorched her throat like acid and she could feel every cell of her body tingle.

Suddenly; a noise to her left attracted her attention. The castle door was ajar and the ringed handle was swinging. She hesitated; she stuffed down the fear as far as it would go and braced herself to go inside and listen at the bottom of the stairs. A noise echoed from above, slowly she crept up the stone steps, aware of every footstep. The rooms were empty, she noted with relief. She reached the top floor and could see no evidence of what had made the noise. From the corner of her eye she noticed a heavy curtain moving in the corner. She tiptoed towards it and grasped the thick material, revealing a heavy wooden door with a huge lock and metal ring. The door, opened onto the roof. Who was a baby now? She'd show Danny…

The two boys shrugged and ran after Rebecca. Suddenly, they heard a yell. The three of them followed the direction of the cry and to their amazement saw Megan waving from the top of the tower. She waved frantically and was shouting something, but they couldn't make it out. Her head just peeped above the parapet and her hands waved wildly, pointing down at them. Abruptly, she disappeared. The children looked at each other.

"Could you see that? I thought I saw someone

behind her," said Danny. "What's she playin' at going up there on her own?"

"I dunno… we'd better get up there!" replied George.

They caught up with Rebecca who ran into the castle just ahead of them. They pounded up the stone staircase, panting for breath, reaching the top level exhausted. The door was wide open and snow was flurrying through the gap. They rushed onto the roof to find nothing but footprints.

"Where the hell is she?" asked Danny, exasperated.

"She must be round the other side… we didn't pass her on the stairs," answered Rebecca. George ran round the roof space. There was no sign of her.

"Look!" he exclaimed, "There are her footprints…" he followed them along the wall, like Sherlock Holmes. "But… someone else was here too! Look!"

They looked at the girl's prints, and could see larger ones all around, finishing in a swirl of disturbed snow, indicating a scuffle.

"Oh no! Someone *was* here! And they've taken her!" Rebecca's face crumpled with emotion.

"*Or* chased her! She might've got away!" said George hopefully.

Danny was leaning over the edge of the parapet and looking down to the street below.

"She ain't down there! But look!"

George and Rebecca approached the battlement walls and peered over them. The snow lay in a fresh white carpet across the small courtyard below. Below them was the imprint of an old grille in the cobbles.

The snow had melted and left the image of the round grate, ornately fashioned centuries before, revealing a star shape.

"A star! It must be a clue – too much of a coincidence otherwise!" said George.

"There must be warmth coming from under it to melt the snow. What's under it?"

"Lets go and see… maybe Meg went down to find it too!" suggested Rebecca.

They retreated from the roof, unaware of the fluttering, sleek, black wings above, as a sole magpie landed on the telephone wire opposite.

Wet footprints on the top of the steps had gone unnoticed before in their haste to find Megan. The prints finished at the heavily curtained wall. George dragged back the curtain, revealing another door, missed in their previous search.

"Shall we go in?" whispered Rebecca, nervously.

"We can't do 'owt else, lass, can we?" said George.

The door creaked open revealing a narrow spiral staircase. It plunged into darkness and none of them relished the dangerous descent. The spiral disorientated them and they clung to the wall, to keep their balance. As their eyes became accustomed to the light they could see a chink of dim light from below. A damp, earthy smell infected their nostrils, suggesting a place unseen by daylight for many a year. The stairs ended abruptly and they cannoned into each other, making Rebecca almost lose her balance. A small door was visible; cold, dank air touched their faces with long wintry fingers. The faint light exposed a large space stretching far beneath the tower, heavy shadows lurking beneath the arches. Boxes were stacked up against the walls, so it was hard to judge how large the cellar was.

"It's like a cave… I don't like caves… they make me claustrophobic," whispered Rebecca.

"Meg… Megan… MEG-AN!" shouted Danny. "She ain't 'ere… she'd have called out by now!" he concluded.

"Where do we start next? We still looking for stars… or is it swans again?" asked George.

"Dunno! But let's get weaving; I don't care for it down here!" shuddered Rebecca.

Shafts of ethereal light filtered through the narrow holes of the grille they had seen from above. George instinctively went to stand beneath it.

He reached up to investigate it with his fingers.

"It's a bit hard to see but I can feel a pattern…"

"Here! I've got my mobile! We can use its light to see," cried Danny.

"Well, don't leave me here!" shouted Rebecca, scrambling through the boxes to reach them.

A small indented star was just visible in the metal of the grille.

"Look! One of its points is longer than the others."

"Where is it pointing to?" asked Danny.

"Towards the wall at the back – lets 'ave a look?" answered George.

George scrambled towards the back wall, shrouded in darkening shadow. There were arches stretching along its length, though each one solid with large sandstone blocks.

"So that's a dead end then!" stated Danny.

"It can't be or the sign wouldn't be pointing this way!" argued Rebecca.

She started to look closely at the walls, tracing her palms across each block.

"What's this? I can feel grooves in the stone… bring the mobile closer Danny!"

Nothing happened, but the light from the mobile revealed a delicately carved swan, so small, it was hardly visible.

"We *must* be in the right place!" Rebecca said triumphantly.

George crouched and placed his palm on top of the swan carving, pressing, hitting and pushing it. It did not move. He explored the stones around it and again nothing happened. He knelt on the floor and explored the stones at the base of the wall.

"*Look*, here on the slab, just below the carving!"

They inspected his find obediently. In the dim light they could just make out another carving at the edge of the paving slab. This time there was a relief carving of a star.

He touched the star carefully, to see what might happen. Nothing did, so he pressed down on it with his foot. Again, nothing. So he stamped hard. A grinding noise rumbled around the cellar. George toppled backwards as the slab slid back, revealing steps leading downwards.

"Oh no! We don't have to go down there, do we?" groaned Rebecca. She had just become used to the damp, dark cellar.

"We have to Beccs, it's the only place Megan can have gone… she's not in the cellar, is she?"

The friends peered down into the gloom below. The steps vanished into it. They edged nervously along the uneven floor. The light was muted, making the narrow, low-ceilinged corridor oppressive.

As their eyes adapted to the weak light, they could see the walls were hewn from bare rock. Rebecca huddled close to George, unsure of what lay ahead. The quiet was suddenly shattered as Rebecca squealed and jumped about, waving her hands in front of her face. She had walked into a long thread from a spider's web. She grabbed Danny and gripped him like a vice.

"Gerroff! It's only a spider's web…" cried Danny.

"It's horrible down here… it's dark and spooky and who knows what's in front of us… and now there's spiders too!" she wailed, "I hate spiders! Urgh!"

"Oh give over, it's not so bad… we must be coming out soon," encouraged George, "Remember we're on a hill, so we can't go much further if we're going up, can we?"

The air was foul and stale and did nothing to alleviate the fear that Rebecca was already consumed with. It reminded her of being on the tube train in London… she hated being enclosed below ground. The tunnel emerged into an archway; leading to yet another cellar, similar to the one they had just left.

"What's that noise?" gasped Rebecca. All her worst nightmares were coming to life!

A high pitched sound, like a whirring top, emerged from the shadows. They stopped and held their breath.

Something was moving in the far corner of the cellar. Nothing was visible, but the noise was becoming louder.

There was a flurry of movement as small bats swooped slickly through the cold air towards them. Rebecca screamed and Danny and George protected their heads with their arms. They glided past them down the passage towards the other cellar.

"Urgh!" George shuddered. "Come on... we've got to find Meg..."

They walked tentatively into the cellar, discovering another door. The silence was stagnant. Small scratching noises shattered the silence. The unearthly scrambling noise amplified behind them, sharp claws gouging and scraping the floor. Panic overtook them all and they struggled to heave open the large oak door, all the time looking furtively behind them to see what horrors were coming their way. To their dismay there were at least a dozen small, monkey like gargoyles, scrabbling across the floor towards them. George and Danny pushed the door harder, banging and pushing frantically. Rebecca hammered on the wood, desperately trying to open it wide enough to escape through. Finally, it gave and George and Rebecca scraped through quickly, hauling Danny with them. Two of the creatures seized his leg.

"HELP! They've got me... Aaargh! " he cried, tears pricking the back of his eyes.

He kicked hard, trying to shake off the wizened animals gripping his trousers. George joined in, punching and pushing. A creature fell backwards and as it hit the floor it shattered into a million pieces of sandstone and dust. The other animals were incensed by this and renewed their efforts, shrieking like banshees. George and Danny made a supreme effort to shut the door, closing it with a thud. One of the gargoyles reached through the door as it shut, its scrawny arm shattering into a million stone shards and dust. The boys gasped with relief as they leant against the door.

"Come on! This is getting dangerous. We need to find Megan and the treasure, quick!" George declared.

They turned to mount the steps leading away from the cellar. They entered the under croft of the church, hunting for signs and clues that Megan had been this way too. Although there was no trace of the girl, something else caught George's eye.

"We're back in the church!"

A large, relief carving of a bishop holding his crosier, was clearly visible in the half light.

"There's a swan, on the front of his robe... is it Cuthbert?"

George inspected the carving. Rebecca stepped forward and reached out to touch the swan, inset was a design inlaid with metal. She pressed gently and felt the metal move. With a little effort she was able to manipulate it and it came free. The metal disc revealed its pattern as it lay in her palm.

"This has got to be the key, the one the monk mentioned," said George.

"But I thought the church was rebuilt in Victorian times? It can't be the same as in Henry VIII's time, can it?" argued Danny.

"I think the passage and the undercroft are part of the old church! It must have been an escape route for the monks. They had to protect themselves from Scottish raiders."

"They'd have been better protecting themselves from Henry!" said Rebecca cynically.

George led the way through the cluttered cellar, pushing past stacks of chairs and broken pews until he reached the door to the church. The air was electric with anticipation. Eventually they emerged into the church.

"We might be safer here," whispered Rebecca, "Maybe those things can't come into a holy place?" she added hopefully.

"Don't bet on it…" Danny responded in an equally hushed voice.

George beckoned them, tiptoeing down the aisle to the back of the church. It was silent and the windows cast an eerie translucent glow across the abandoned pews. A wintry light played up and down the aisles like icy threads frozen in time.

George paused at the font, moving to where they had seen the abbot place the treasure. He knelt, examining the stone panels. He fingered the carving and a smile broke across his face like sunshine on a cloudy day.

"Look! It's the abbey emblem… and I think the disc fits over it. All the bumpy bits match the holes in it!"

George placed the disc on top of the carving, manoeuvring it until it fitted perfectly. He pushed it down and then twisted it; slowly it began to turn. The lower section of the panel rose, revealing a secret chamber in the bottom of the font.

A package lay inside.

"It's now or never…" George drew it carefully from its hiding place.

The package was heavy with the dust of centuries. George placed it carefully on the floor. Rebecca stared and Danny took a deep breath. They could not believe the treasure was in their grasp at last.

"Shall I open it?" he asked in a whisper.

"Watch out! Don't let him!" a squeal from behind a pillar made them spin around, just in time to see Megan, held by Mr Steele.

"That will be my privilege, young man!"

Steele and Megan had appeared from nowhere.

"If you want your little friend back, I suggest you put the package on the floor. Now!"

The boys flashed a look at each other. Steele smiled menacingly.

"I wouldn't do anything rash, if I were you! Put the package down!"

There was no alternative but to obey.

He pushed Megan forcefully towards them, causing George and Danny to stumble and fall. Rebecca ran towards the parcel, but Steele was quicker than a scorpion's sting. He swept up the package and made a dart for the door in one easy, fluid movement.

The children scrambled to take up the chase, a scratching sound heralded the arrival of several skittering gargoyles, scurrying like spiders along the aisles towards them. Stone ground against stone as the carved creatures crunched along the floor. George ducked behind the font. The screaming assault came from all sides and they tried to fight the creatures off with anything that came to hand. Danny clunked two with the brass ewer; they instantly exploded into rubble and dust at a touch. This emboldened Rebecca and George, grabbing Megan's arm, they rushed for the door; the creatures shrieked with a high pitched whine as they launched themselves at the children once more. George hit out as hard as he could, with some candlesticks, Rebecca and Megan with the heavy, brass collection plate. With each strike, gargoyles smashed against the walls and floor, shattering, like falling Christmas baubles. Finally, they escaped through the church door and onto the path.

The snow was still falling heavily, everything silent and muffled. The street and the square were empty. They looked round to see where Steele had gone, but there was no sign of him.

"He's there!" Danny pointed down the hill.

"He's going down the ginnel, let's get after him."

"No! We can go past the Brown Cow! It's a short cut!" said Rebecca.

They slipped and slid in the soft snow as they went, all the way to the bottom of the hill. Steele dashed past the pinfold, racing towards the "Haggs". His heavy burden slowed him down and George and Danny gained on him. He disappeared into the short tunnel under the railway line. The going was hard, the snow quite deep by now, covering the path, obscuring the ditches and the dips. Megan stumbled and fell and was immediately pulled to her feet again by Rebecca.

Steele fled swiftly along the narrow snow covered path, his coat flying behind like a black sail. Birds above them swooped, screeching alarmingly, black and blue feathers blotting the white backdrop of the snow. George and Danny threw sticks and rocks to chase them away. Their anxiety rose like a tsunami, time was running out…

"We've got to stop him! He's going to the abbey he'll escape back to his own time from there! " shouted George, urgently.

They ran on and on, panting, chests bursting with the effort. Steele turned towards the west gate. They darted across the main road, dipping and dodging in and out of the slow moving line of cars, struggling to make it up the hill.

As George and Rebecca skidded to the top of the path, Steele fell. He lost his grip on the package and it flew into the crisp, cold air, suspended for a brief moment. George leaped forward to catch it, as easily as if it was a rugby ball. He rolled as he caught the parcel and slid a few feet across the snow, ploughing a furrow. Steele slowly rose from his landing place, looking stunned.

George recovered from his fall, clutching the parcel. Steele faced him and his top lip curled back menacingly. He glowered at the boy and stretched out his hand to retrieve the treasure.

"You will return my property boy! NOW!" he snarled.

"NEVER! It belonged to the abbey and it should be somewhere safe!" retorted George.

Steele lunged at George and tried to grab the precious treasure. Danny was spurred into action and rushed to his aid. The girls glanced at each other and simultaneously lunged at the defenceless man. A struggle ensued and each one battled hard to protect George and the sacred treasure. The man's face reddened with fury, he howled like a wounded animal, but Danny and the two girls pounded him relentlessly.

Abruptly, Steele jolted backwards as if he had been electrocuted. He fell to the ground and lay prone, unable to move. A tall, familiar figure stood behind them. John Stell stood looking more real and solid than he had ever done. He observed Steele sadly, a little like a disappointed parent.

"My son, leave these children to fulfil their quest. The treasure is not thine and can never be. It must not be used for ill. Ye have betrayed me and our kinsmen and put the treasure at risk of being lost to man forever."

Steele shrank and cringed as he stared at the monk, trembling in fear.

"You are no kin to me old monk! You are long past; you are my imagination playing tricks..."

"You know he is the guardian, Ambrose Steele... your line is the same as his... the same as Thomas Snell... you are the rotten branch of your tree, you cannot win!" interjected Mason, who appeared mysteriously from behind Brother John.

"Go back Ambrose and let the treasure be," said the familiar voice of Mrs Rogers. She materialised beside her brother and the old monk, "Your power is weakening…"

The man's eyes darted from one to the other like a hunted animal, his pathway blocked by the triangle of good souls. They moved towards him, closing his means of escape. George slyly moved backwards, away from Steele, but a cawing noise arose from the birds perched on the ruined archway of the gate. Steele used the momentary distraction to seize the package, breaking through the protective wall that John Stell and his friends had cast around the children.

He sped, slipping and sliding across the car park and disappeared into the museum. George reached the door first but his path was blocked by the cashier. She locked the door, smiling malevolently through the glass. George could just see the black tails of Steele's coat disappearing into the grounds. Danny and Rebecca pushed against the door. The woman sniggered and wagged a finger at them. Slowly the expression on her face altered. Her eyes grew wide and her face grew ashen. Stell had emerged behind them. She dropped her keys and staggered back into the museum. She turned and fled, disappearing from view completely.

"C'mon! Over the fence!" yelled George.

The monk had disappeared; it was left to the children to solve the problem alone.

They scrambled over the fence, falling into the soft snow on the other side. Steele was running across the nave towards the cloisters. They ran for all they were worth, sliding and stumbling as they went.

George raced out in front; he could not bear to

think that the treasure would be lost to him again. They followed him down towards the Chapter House. Steele was trapped like a fox in a snare; the Chapter House was one of the few places in the abbey which had retained its walls.

He snarled, grimacing and held the precious package close to his chest.

"You will never take this from me again! I have waited for years, it will give me fame... and riches beyond my wildest dreams... and the power to move through time, taking what I will and finding refuge in other places... I deserve it... its mi..."

"It isn't yours Mr Steele! I won't let you have it... neither will George or Danny and Meg... you don't belong here... your time is over..." Rebecca asserted bravely.

The others stared incredulously at her. What did she think she could do to prevent Steele?

"My time is just beginning... it's another chance for me!" he snapped.

"No! You don't belong here... give up the treasure."

"That boy doesn't belong here either, or Mason and his sister, or Stell... why shouldn't I have the prize?" He pleaded pathetically, like a small child who had been denied sweets.

"No but you prevent them from leaving...you have no power here... we are too strong... Cuthbert wills it..." she spoke trance like. Her friends could not believe she had spoken the words; it was as if she was possessed by a greater being, an older soul. What she had said invoked something supernatural.

A luminous white light rose from the package. Steele dropped it as if it had burnt him. The light hovered above the ground, swelling in intensity and size. Steele cowered terrified, shrinking visibly in front of them. Rebecca stood immobile. Her face was as tranquil and peaceful as an alabaster statue. Within the light, shapes flickered and flashed, a series of pictures forming and then vanishing. The light rapidly intensified and from its heart evolved a superlative, silvery swan.

The friends gasped at its beauty and brilliance. The light emanating from it was dazzling. Its long, strong neck arched gracefully and it raised its huge regal wings, flapping them slowly and widely. As it rose to its full height, it towered over the wretched Steele. The air froze and everyone was powerless to move. The swan stretched its wings to their widest span, each delicate feather quivering with silver energy. Steele was swallowed by the light radiating from the swan. Its brilliance was amplified for a fleeting moment, power surging and simultaneously an anguished cry rose from where Steele had been standing. The light faded and flickered like a guttering candle. The swan and Steele were gone.

All that was left was the package, pressed into the newly laid snow.

CHAPTER 20

GOODBYE

The children silently surrounded the package. Although they had hated Steele for trying to steal the treasure, they felt sorry that he had left this world in such terror. Megan wept quietly, Rebecca looked bemused and dazed, even George and Danny were pensive and quiet. Nobody moved and then a fluttering wind disturbed the snow. John Stell was with them.

"Worry not about Ambrose; he is but returned to his own time and must serve penance for his greed, but as with all men, he will find forgiveness when his time ends. Ye have saved a precious and powerful treasure for all men. These good folk are released from their troubles and will return to their own time," he indicated Mason and Mrs Rogers who had also re-appeared.

Together, they unwrapped the fragile leather bindings carefully, the treasure was at last revealed.

"It's a book..." whispered Rebecca.

The book was bound in leather, worked and fashioned by a craftsman long dead. The pages were beautifully illuminated, the colours looking as fresh as they had when they were first created. A Latin inscription stood bold on the first page, its capital letter entwined with a beautiful swan.

"I think it says Cuthbert… something…"

"It must be dead old then!" said Danny.

"It's a Bible, there are pictures… Adam and Eve, Noah and… wow!" gasped Rebecca.

"It must be priceless! No wonder Steele wanted it! He would have made a fortune… hey, we're rich!" Danny piped up.

George shook his head.

"No Danny, it's not to make us rich. It is for everyone to share isn't that right, Mr Mason?"

"Yes, but we will be richer, knowing this is safe and its power can't be used to change time or used for evil."

Events after Christmas became a whirl. Questions had been asked which were very difficult to answer and it hadn't helped that George had vanished again.

Cuthbert's Bible had been placed in the British Library, a new treasure for the nation. It had been such a significant find that everyone heard of it world wide. The rare Bible was as important as the Stonyhurst Gospel, which had been buried with him. It had accompanied the saint on his seven year journey, when his monks carried his coffin to safety away from Lindisfarne. Of course, few people knew of the book's hidden supernatural power.

Their photos had been in the newspapers, they had appeared on *Northwest Tonight* and they enjoyed their brief time of celebrity. Like everything, this soon passed and became a memory. The children slipped easily back into their old lives. Mason promised he would see them again, but was now free to return to his real life. The book would be cared for by others who knew of its magnitude.

They walked to the abbey for a last look before school started again in January. The snow had begun to melt and everything looked weather beaten and bedraggled. At the bottom of the lane a familiar figure appeared on Bow Bridge. It was George, grinning widely.

The winter mist swirled in from the Irish Sea and rolled across the valley bottom. The cold and damp struck the children through their shoes and they shivered. It was a relief that the day had been won, but it was strange realising that the adventure was over. Danny spoke first, "Well, George, we thought you'd gone for good. D'ya wanna come back with us?"

George smiled slowly, shaking his head.

"No ta! I've got to go, I only came to say bye... I've finished what I started and it's time I went..."

Rebecca looked straight at him. The back of her eyes prickled with tears, not yet cried. He looked back at her with a solemnity far older than his years.

"We're not going to see you again are we?" she whispered, the words catching in her throat.

"Well... you never know... one day..." his voice trailed off, his bright blue eyes glistening with moistness.

"But where are you going? Why can't we see you again?" she demanded, already knowing the answer.

"I'm going "home". We've been lucky, we had more time than we should, everything has to end sometime, and every day was a bonus..." That was just what Granddad used to say when he wasn't feeling too good.

He held open his arms and Rebecca ran to hug him.

For a few seconds she glowed with warmth and security. His arms were strong and protective around her. She was safe and calm for the first time in many weeks. He squeezed her hard and then broke away gently. He looked straight into her eyes and smiled a little sadly.

He turned to the boys and slapped them on the back and gently hugged Megan. Sighing, he pushed his hands in his pockets and hunched his shoulders. He slowly turned and looked back at them smiling, pulling his cap from his pocket and tugging it down over his head. He tapped the peak of the cap and grinned again, saying, "So long, then! I'm glad we saved the treasure… I've waited a long time to do it…" he turned away again and began walking down the path. Mist billowed and enveloped his slight form.

Rebecca caught her breath and ran towards him. She called out, anxiously. She felt a pain inside, a pain she had experienced before.

"But George… I don't want you to go yet!"

He stopped, almost obscured by the grey mist now. As he turned around, he shouted back, "I know. You'll see me again… one day…" and waved again.

The boy disappeared into the mist, his silhouette fading. The children stared at the space he had occupied and Rebecca put her hand to her mouth in anticipation.

Slowly, a slight breeze fluttered, disturbing fallen leaves along the pathway. The flurry of cold, damp air played with the hanging mist and momentarily pushed it out of the way, revealing the boy, still waving. The fingers of fog playfully flicked around his form, obscuring him again. Rebecca took a deep breath, transfixed by his image. She almost stopped breathing altogether as she saw George start to walk away, very slowly and ponderously. As he moved away, he leaned heavily on his stick. Rebecca's mouth fell open.

The boy was no longer there. Instead, a familiar and much loved figure walked away. She couldn't help herself. She ran forward a few steps, but then stopped almost immediately. He stopped and turned back to look at her. He shook his head, sadly and smiled. The old man pulled up the collar of his beige jacket and tugged down the peak of his old battered, trilby hat. He walked slowly, leaning on his stick, into the mist. As he reached the trees, he turned once again and waved. Rebecca couldn't speak, a large lump rose in her throat, as the truth dawned on her. George stopped again. Granddad… and their co-crusader… one and the same.

As she looked, a familiar robed figure appeared behind him, beckoning. He appeared to be illuminated by a brilliant white light behind him, just like the one that had emanated from the swan. George waved again and walked towards the light, diminishing and changing as he did so. The boy appeared for a second, turning and running, then, the old man was there in his stead… silhouetted against the ever increasing light. The light narrowed to a tiny sliver and then vanished in an instant. A small ethereal white butterfly fluttered and danced and then was gone.

Rebecca's face was damp with silent tears. But sadness was now tinged with hope. Her parting from

George was painful just like the first time, but now she knew that she *would* see him again... one day. She understood why the boy had seemed so familiar now. Why had she not realised sooner? There were so many things she could have, *would have* asked him? She hadn't even noticed the name – Granddad's "Sunday" name, "George"! She had always known that Sam was his nickname, called after an old football player... how had she not realised?

Megan came up behind her and put her arm round her. She hugged her.

"Don't get upset... George will be fine, he's got to go back to his time... we might see him again..."

"Yeah... but... no! Didn't you see what happened...?"

"Yes, he ran off up the path and then we couldn't see him because of the mist..."

"But... he changed..."

"What *are* you on about?"

Suddenly, Rebecca realised they had not seen what she had seen. That would be her memory and nobody else's. She knew now what Mason had meant when their adventure had started, when he said that you can be real, but not necessarily alive. She had *so* wanted to see Granddad again. She had hoped it would make her feel better. Even though she was crying, she didn't feel as desolate as she had when he had first died... because she knew that he was still there. He was still around, not visible, but there just the same.

He would be there always, waiting. One day they would meet again, and be reunited in the special place where he now was. She knew that he would always be with her, hidden in her heart even though he couldn't be seen. It made her feel better, like he was away on holiday and he would come back sometime soon. She decided to keep this to herself; it would be her own secret. Her own secret treasure, her own precious treasure.

AUTHOR'S NOTE

Out of Time is a story woven around a very beautiful area called the Furness peninsula, tucked away in the north west of England. Many of the places mentioned are real and can be visited. Furness Abbey is a spectacular Cistercian abbey, built in 1127 on land gifted by King Stephen to monks from Savigny. It was one of the richest abbeys in England and its lands covered the Furness area reaching as far as Cumberland. It was the first abbey to be dissolved by Henry VIII probably because of its vast wealth. The ruins we see today are magnificent, but the fabric of the church is in danger because the oak rafts it was built upon are degenerating and tilting. It would be tragic if the abbey were to finally fall completely, after surviving Henry's plundering, years of local people "robbing" out the stones to build new structures and acid rain damaging the stone during the recent century. English Heritage is the custodian and they are working to repair the damage.

Many legends surround St Cuthbert and I have tried to reflect these in this story. He is linked to numerous stories and miracles and has a number of emblems; the swan is one of these.

The story is set against three historical timelines. I have tried to be accurate with real events and have included the names of real people. I have however, used my imagination, entwining the legends I heard as a child, to create the quest.

The characters all have some basis in truth; the present day characters are disguised, but those in the past are real. John Stell truly existed and lived and worked as a scribe at the abbey, Thomas Holcroft was an officer of Henry VIII, who dissolved the abbey, stripping it of its assets. The Abbots' names and details are taken from evidence from the Furness Coucher Books. I owe some of the facts I use to the diligent scholarship of Alice Leach an eminent local historian, who loves the abbey as much as I do.

The tale of the ghost and the delivery boy was told to me by my Dad, who takes most credit for my characterisation of George. It was he who first introduced me to the abbey and inspired me to love history, so it is to him I dedicate this book.